the secret of the rose

The Secret of the ROSE

Sarah L. Thomson

Sarah L. Thomson

Nov. 2006

GREENWILLOW BOOKS
An Imprint of HarperCollins*Publishers*

The Secret of the Rose

Copyright © 2006 by Sarah L. Thomson

All rights reserved. No part of this book may be used or reproduced in any manner whatsoever without written permission except in the case of brief quotations embodied in critical articles and reviews. Printed in the United States of America. For information address HarperCollins Children's Books, a division of HarperCollins Publishers, 1350 Avenue of the Americas, New York, NY 10019.

www.harperchildrens.com

The text of this book is set in AGaramond.

Book design by Paul Zakris

Library of Congress Cataloging-in-Publication Data

Thomson, Sarah L.

The secret of the Rose / by Sarah L. Thomson.

   p. cm.

"Greenwillow Books."

Summary: When her father is imprisoned in 1592 England for being Catholic, fourteen-year-old Rosalind disguises herself as a boy and finds an ultimately dangerous job as servant to playwright Christopher Marlowe.

ISBN-10: 0-06-087250-0 (trade bdg.) ISBN-13: 978-0-06-087250-2 (trade bdg.)

ISBN-10: 0-06-087251-9 (lib. bdg.) ISBN-13: 978-0-06-087251-9 (lib. bdg.)

[1. Sex roles—Fiction. 2. Survival—Fiction. 3. Theater—Fiction. 4. Catholics—England—History—16th century—Fiction. 5. Marlowe, Christopher, 1564-1593—Fiction. 6. Rose Theatre—Fiction. 7. London (England)—History—16th century—Fiction. 8. Great Britain—History—Elizabeth, 1558-1603—Fiction.] I. Title.

PZ7.T378Sec 2006 [Fic]—dc22 2005022177

First Edition 10 9 8 7 6 5 4 3 2 1

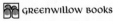 GREENWILLOW BOOKS

For Ric, with thanks and love
—s. l. t.

Thanks to Susan Tananbaum
for her help and advice

august 1592

〜

They put the heads of traitors on spikes over the gate of London Bridge.

"They boil 'em first," said a woman's voice from behind us in the jostling crowd. "And dip 'em in tar."

"Oh, aye," another voice answered her with ghoulish satisfaction. "Makes 'em last longer. They do say some of 'em have been up there ten years and more. Take care, then—"

That last part was to me, for I had stopped in the middle of the road, putting out a hand to clutch my brother by the arm. The two women pushed past, grumbling. People walked around Robin and me as we stood, looking up at the great stone gatehouse with a tower three stories tall rising over the arched entrance to the bridge. On the top of the tower, in the red-gold light just before sunset, we could see the long poles with the blackened heads. They had no faces anymore, but it was too easy to imagine the hollow eyes watching us, the empty mouths stretched open in silent warning.

"Rosalind?" Robin asked me, very quietly. "Will they do that to Father?"

"Of course not!" It was a relief to be angry, to let my anger set my feet moving again. "That's for traitors. Father's no traitor, Robin."

"But he—"

"Peace, Robin!" The crowd was pressing in close on either side as we squeezed underneath the gate and onto the bridge, and it would not do to talk in public of what our father had done. Or of the evening I had been picking rosemary in the garden. I'd come into the kitchen, my hands full of the small, sweet-smelling leaves, and had heard voices. Peering into the hallway, I saw my father standing at the open front door. Outside, holding a lantern, was Thomas Chapman, the sheriff.

"'Tis late for a visit, Tom," my father had said mildly.

"I have no choice in the matter, Master Archer."

From where I stood, hesitating at the end of the long, dark passage, I could see other men behind the sheriff, men that I knew.

"You'll let us in, Master Archer," the sheriff said.

"Indeed," my father answered, looking out at our

friends and neighbors, come to tear our lives apart. "It seems I have no choice as well."

No, it would not do to talk about it now.

I kept tight hold of the sack over my shoulder that held everything I owned in the world and took Robin by the hand. Normally this was a thing he would not allow, now that he was all of ten and disdained mothering by his older sister. But he did not let go, and swung his own sack with his other hand as we made our way across the bridge, wide as a street, with shops lining either side. The air was damp with the heat of late summer, and heavy with the stench of the River Thames below.

Apprentices were closing the stores for the night, clearing off the goods from the wooden shutters, hinged at the bottom, that could be let down into the street to form counters. But as I passed by a glove maker's, my eye lingered on a white pair sewn with pansies. In an instant a boy Robin's age, eager for one last sale, snatched the gloves up and held them out to me. "Very pretty, mistress, and soft as a kitten's fur, just feel this now, and the height of the fashion . . ."

Shaking my head, I gripped Robin's hand and walked on. It was true I had money in my purse, hanging from the girdle beneath my petticoats for safekeeping. But it was not for luxuries like new gloves. The Rosalind Archer of two weeks ago, daughter of a rich merchant, might have fancied such vanities. But the Rosalind Archer of today had different uses for her money.

There was another tall gatehouse to walk under at the far end of the bridge, and then we were in London itself.

This city, I thought, was bursting at its seams. The buildings crowded together, shoulder to shoulder: houses, taverns, inns with their bold wooden signs, fishmongers, the pavement before them slick and bright with blood and silver scales. Even the air was crammed full of noise. "Fish! Freshest fish!" bellowed the shopkeepers, and women with baskets on their arms argued shrilly over prices. Someone laughed and chattered to a companion in a language I had never heard. The breath in my nose was thick with smells—the filth of the river, horse dung in the street, meat cooking in the taverns, the sour tang of beer, and the strong, salty, rotten stink of fish.

I felt battered and shaken and breathless. My feet, of their own accord, faltered and stopped once more. How did anyone ever find their way in this maze, this din, this absurd mass of people? In my panic, all I wanted was to turn and run, back across the bridge, back down the country roads Robin and I had trudged so wearily, back to the village where I knew every house, every face, where I practically knew every sheep in the fields.

Foolish. Impossible. Oh, the village was still there, the

houses and the fields and no doubt the sheep as well. But there would be no returning, either for Robin or for me. And hadn't I learned in these past weeks that the men and women I had grown up among were as much strangers to me as the people pushing past us in this unfamiliar street?

I took a breath to steady myself. We had nowhere to return to. But we did have somewhere to go. We had come to this overwhelming city for a reason—to find our father. And when we did, it would not matter that we were strangers here, that we were lost. Because when we found him, then we would be home.

"Rosalind," Robin said impatiently, dropping my hand. "Why dost thou stand there? We must . . ." I could not hear the rest of his sentence as he pushed his way forward into the crowd. In a heartbeat he was lost to my sight.

Lost to me.

Fighting down a spike of panic, I shoved my way after him, looking everywhere for a tall, skinny boy with a crop of brown curls and a green doublet with striped sleeves. I saw nothing. "Mind thyself!" someone said impatiently, and I was pushed to one side. I was not tall enough to see over the heads of the people before me. Where had he gone? Peering frantically left and right, I walked straight into the person in front of me and all but broke my nose on the back of his skull.

"Rosalind!" Robin complained, rubbing his head. "Canst not watch where thou'rt walking?"

"Robin!" I could have shaken him for giving me such a fright. "Art mad? Stay close to me!" And I seized hold of his sleeve.

My brother's jaw tightened, and his face took on the stubborn look I knew, to my sorrow, very well. It was a look that went with his old complaint: *Let me be. I need not obey thee. Thou'rt not my mother.*

Well, I may not have been his mother, but I was the closest thing he had to one, since our mother had not lived two hours after his birth. I had raised him from a swaddled babe, and he might have given me some gratitude, if not obedience. But I knew better than to expect it.

Now he twitched his sleeve free of my grasp and scowled at me. "God's teeth, thou'rt worse than a mother hen," he grumbled. "Thou'rt not my nurse."

"Then do not act as if thou needst one," I snapped. "We've no time to waste traipsing about London."

"'Twas *thou* standing like a stone in the street," Robin pointed out. "I was not the one idling away our time."

"Thou dost not even know the way."

"Nor dost thou!"

Saints preserve me from little brothers, I thought, and turned my attention to a woman walking past. Her hair, dark as a Spaniard's, was tucked under an elegant velvet hat. "Pray, mistress," I said to her. She didn't even turn her head to look at us. "Pray, sir—" I tried a little louder with a man striding by on our other side, in the long gown of a scholar. He glanced aside, sniffed, and walked quicker.

"What needst thou, lass?" someone asked kindly.

But the kindness didn't stop me from turning with a rebuke sharp on my tongue. The woman who'd spoken was clearly a servant, in a plain, patched gown, fish tails poking out of the basket over her arm. How dared she use the familiar "thou" to me, as if she were my equal?

Then I bit back the words on their way out of my mouth and saw myself as I must look to her: unwashed and footsore, dusty from the road, curls of brown hair straggling down beneath my coif, lost in a strange town without a man or maid to attend me. In truth, I did not appear to be someone that even a servant should address with a respectful "you."

So I swallowed my hard words and my pride along with them, although the taste was bitter in my mouth, and answered civilly, "We are looking for Chancery Lane."

"Ah, well then, thou hast a fair bit of walking still to do." She pointed up the hill before us, into the heart of London. "Dost see the crossroads ahead? Turn west there and walk along Westcheape and Watling, through

Ludgate. Then thou'lt be in Fleet Street, and thou must turn right into Chancery." I blinked in confusion at the unfamiliar names, and she smiled. "Never fear, lass, thou'lt find thy way."

I was not so sure of that, but I thanked her, and Robin and I set out through London.

We left the fish markets behind as we turned west, and we made our way among the crowds, keeping near the houses and shops as carts and wagons clattered down the center of the street. This time Robin kept close to me. "Is all London like this?" he asked.

"Ah, Robin, how should I know? Father used to speak of it. . . ." When Father came home from selling his wool in London, he'd have money in his purse and gifts for Robin and me: lace for my petticoat, buckles for Robin's shoes, sweet gingerbread. He'd sweep us both up in a hug to crush our ribs, declaring that he'd missed us terribly, that he'd wept for grief every night. And then he'd laugh and tell how he had been to the playhouse to watch *Tamburlaine* with the grand swordfights or seen the famous bear, Tom of Lincoln, triumph over five dogs at the baiting.

He had never talked about crowds that seemed to use up all the air, or streets that twisted like a maze, or heads on spikes over London Bridge.

I hurried Robin along as the light began to fade, not even sparing much of a glance for the huge stone bulk of St. Paul's Cathedral as we passed by. I'd no wish to be out on the streets after nightfall. We must reach Chancery Lane before dark. There, I thought with gratitude and relief, would be refuge and safety and some sort of peace. All things that had been sorely lacking since the night Sheriff Chapman had come to our door.

When we did arrive at last, I saw that Chancery Lane was a quieter street than the ones we had just walked through. The houses looked freshly plastered and prosperous. "Which is it?" Robin asked.

"I know no more than thee. We must ask again."

"Hurry, then." Before I could put out a hand to stop him, Robin had darted away to a tavern, where a group of young men stood talking and laughing under the hanging sign.

I would not have chosen to ask the way of men gathered outside a tavern door. But Robin was already speaking to one of them as I approached.

"Do you know the house of John Eastfield?" he asked.

"Eastfield?" The man who answered had a thick country accent. "Na, there be no Eastfields here." Someone in the group sniggered, as if it were a joke.

"But—'tis Chancery Lane? Our father said—"

"John Eastfield is a friend of my father," I said with dignity. They were trying to have a joke with us, it seemed. No doubt they would think it amusing to misdirect strangers. "He has lived in this street these past five years."

"Aye, that he has. But he lives here no more."

It was a second man who spoke, wearing apprentice's blue. I had never seen eyes like his before, a sharp light gray, so pale that they seemed almost no color at all. They went oddly with his thick black brows and hair.

"Has the family moved?" I asked, uncertain.

"Aye, moved into prison."

Oh, sweet saints . . .

"The law came for them just last week. Papists, the lot of them. Wife and children, too." All the men in the crowd were staring at us now.

"Papists?" I gasped. I knew I must seem horrified, and my real shock made the act convincing. "How dreadful! My father had some business with the man, but he never thought. . . ." My voice died under the pressure of the bright interest in the watching eyes. And after all, why should I explain myself to them? "Come," I told Robin. There was low laughter behind us as we turned.

Run. My heart was thumping a command to my blood. *Run. They've guessed. They know—*

But my head overruled the order. There might still be

The garden was walled, no one in it but ourselves. Joan, our maidservant, was singing in the kitchen, too occupied with the sound of her own voice to listen for ours. Yet he kept his voice low. Walls have chinks. I'd learned very young that anyone might be listening.

"If aught happens to me, there are friends who will help thee," he'd said. And he'd named them and made me repeat the names. The Masons the next village over. The Eyres in the market town. John Eastfield and his family, away to the south, on Chancery Lane in London.

I had not dared to go to the Masons. They were too close to our own village, and too well known as friends of our father. The Eyres had hidden us for two nights but feared to keep us longer. People knew what my father had done; anyone found harboring his children would fall under suspicion as well.

The Eastfields had been my last hope. Now who would take us in?

"Rosalind!"

"Lower thy voice!" My own was shaking. "We must . . . we must go to an inn, that is all, Robin. And tomorrow we'll see Father. He'll tell us what to do."

If there was no one to take us in, we would have to find work of some sort. I had money in my purse, but not enough to keep us forever, and in any case it was money I had meant to help our father, not spend on our own needs.

Robin was old enough to hire out as an apprentice. And I . . . well, I could at the very worst find a servant's place. My lip curled a little at the thought of brushing clothes and scrubbing floors. But I would do it, if need be. If it was the only way to help our father.

Robin let out his breath at my words. "Aye, Father will know." He was frightened, too, I realized. I should not have spoken so sharply to him. "Which way, then?" he asked.

A very good question. The street had narrowed so that the upper stories of the houses almost blocked out what little light there was. We'd left the crowds behind. Except for a pig rooting through the garbage that filled the gutter, Robin and I were alone.

I looked ahead, trying to see Ludgate or the old city wall, but did not succeed. Robin smirked. "Thou dost not know the way?"

"Well, at Ludgate we can ask again." But surely we should have reached the gate by now. I began to wonder if we'd gone the wrong way.

"Art lost, then?"

I turned, my heart giving a sudden painful jolt under my ribs. There behind us was the apprentice who'd given us directions. Now his smile was broader and there was another man with him, one eye drooping in a squint that gave him an evil leer.

I took a step backward. "No, I thank you. All's well."

"I told thee to turn at the surgeon's. Didst not attend?"

"No, you told us—" I faltered, looking at those pale eyes. "Robin, run," I whispered.

But I'd left it too late. Even as I spun around to flee, his hand grasped my arm and yanked, and I fell sprawling to the muddy street. I heard Robin cry out, with rage or maybe pain, I couldn't tell. The hand on my arm pulled me up, but I could not find my balance to resist as he dragged me, stumbling, half falling, into a gap between two houses.

He threw me down on my back and was kneeling beside me, one hand pinning my shoulder to the ground, the other fumbling at my skirts. Behind him I could see that the man with the squint had hold of Robin, one hand over his mouth, the other twisting an arm cruelly behind his back. "Why all this fuss, then?" the apprentice panted, his cheeks flushed red. His hot, damp breath in my face was sour, with a smell of stale wine, and his pale eyes were at once clouded and shining, like thick, murky glass. "Why dost wander the streets alone, speaking to men, shameless, if thou dost not want—"

He stopped. My skirts were above my knees, his hand groping up my bare leg. "What's this?" A slow grin spread over his face. "There's more here—" His hand closed around the heavy purse that hung from my girdle and wrenched it free.

"No!" I shrieked. Shock and terror had stolen my tongue until that moment, but that he should take my money—*our* money—money I needed, if I were ever to help my father—was enough to move me to action.

I thrashed against his hand, kicking wildly. He was still staring at the purse he now held, astonished at its weight. One of my feet caught him in the ribs, and the other, more by luck than by planning, squarely between his legs. He doubled over, clutching himself and letting out a short, startled moan. I scrambled to my feet just as the man holding Robin let him go and darted forward to seize the purse from his companion's unresisting fingers.

"Run!" I shouted to Robin.

In fact, I do not think they chased us. The man with the squint may have been satisfied with what he'd already gained; the man I had kicked was not likely to chase anything. But at the time I did not think of that, or even look behind me to see if anyone was following. I only ran blindly, around corners, down more narrow side streets, through squares and alleys, ducking and pushing through crowds, hardly noticing whether Robin was with me. I felt as if those pale eyes were just behind me, that rough hand reaching out for me, that mocking voice in my ear. *Art lost, then?*

When at last I had to stop for want of breath, we were in another narrow, winding street; I had no notion which one. But it was fairly full of people, even in the gathering darkness. It seemed safe.

My knees wouldn't hold me. I sat down abruptly by the side of the road, not caring how filthy the ground was or what would become of my already stained skirts.

Robin crouched beside me. His skinny face was pinched with remorse. "Rosalind? Art hurt? I am sorry, I could not. . . ."

He was sorry. My little brother, four years younger, was sorry he could not save me from two grown men, each easily twice his size. A sob came from somewhere near my heart. How could Robin protect me? He was only a boy. He should be swimming in the river back home, or planning ways to disrupt Master Crabbe's lessons in Latin grammar, or running races with the friends who wouldn't talk to him now that they knew the truth of what he was. He should not be trying to save me from men who wanted—who wanted—

And now our money was gone. The friends we'd hoped

to find had been taken. We were lost in London. Robin could not keep me safe, and neither could Father. No one would help us.

Wooden cartwheels and horse's hooves passed us by. Feet in buckled shoes or high boots or wooden clogs walked indifferently along. No doubt their owners saw worse things every day than a bedraggled girl crying by the roadside and her brother patting her shoulder in awkward comfort.

chapter two
august 1592

But after a time I had to be done crying at last, and dry my face on my sleeve, and take stock of myself. Robin and I were sitting in a dark and dirty street, in front of a small draper's shop, the shutters now closed tightly for the night. My shoulder ached, and I was sore and stiff on hip and elbow where I'd landed on the cobblestones, but other than that I was not hurt. I brushed helplessly at the muddy patches on my skirts, to no effect. I would just have to be filthy until I found a way to be clean again.

"Rosalind?" Robin was still peering at me anxiously. "Art hurt? That man?"

"Do not speak of it."

"But he—"

"Do not speak of it!" Although I had stopped crying, my voice still frayed around the edges, and sympathy from my pest of a little brother was likely to start the tears again. I did not want to talk about the man with the pale gray eyes; I did not want to think about him. Frantically I cast about for something else to occupy my thoughts. "Thy sack, Robin," I demanded. "Where is it?"

"I—" Robin looked down, as if startled, at his empty hands.

"Didst drop it?"

"Thou didst as well!"

I realized he was right; my sack was gone also. In it had been the few things I'd managed to save from home—an ivory comb, my scissors, a packet of needles and thread, a coral necklace, a warm winter cloak with a fur-lined hood. Well, it would be some little time before I'd be needing that, at least.

"'Twas not my fault," Robin said, a little angrily.

"No," I agreed with a sigh. "Never mind it. Art hurt? Thine arm?"

"No." He rubbed at his arm gingerly. "'Tis nothing. I'm fine."

"Dost still have the purse I gave thee?"

Robin's eyes widened with eagerness. "Yes! I have it here!"

"Do not take it out!" Robin's hand dropped away from his belt, where our second purse hung, hidden inside his loose breeches. It did not hold much, not nearly as much as the one I had carried. But I'd thought it wise to give him a few shillings in case we were separated. I was not even sure it would be enough for a night at the cheapest inn. But it would keep us from begging for a day or two.

Tears welled up again, and I tipped my head back and squeezed my eyes shut tight to keep them from overflowing.

Robin tugged at my arm. "Rosalind?"

"Leave me be," I whispered. We'd lost our home, we'd lost our friends, and now we'd lost our money, too. We'd hardly anything left.

"Rosalind!" Robin insisted.

Annoyance with my brother was such a comforting, familiar emotion. I turned to him, opening my eyes again. "What is't! Why must thou—"

He pointed over my shoulder.

Behind me, the draper whose shop we were sitting in front of waved a broom. "Be off!" he commanded. "Or I'll call the watch on you. Vagabonds, idle, wretched—"

Robin was on his feet, and I jumped up, too, and clutched at his shoulder, pulling him away before the angry shopkeeper could have the law on us. Safely around the corner, I stopped, hesitating, and looked back. The man did not seem to have followed, satisfied with having swept us away from his shop like trash into the gutter.

"Where will we go?" Robin asked me.

Must I always decide? I looked around helplessly.

"We've no money for an inn."

As if I did not know it. But where, in this terrible city, could we find a safe place for the night, somewhere we would not be turned out by a shopkeeper or householder, somewhere the law would not take us in for vagabonds, to be flogged and branded and sent on our way, as if we had anywhere to go?

Something caught my eye. "There," I said, pointing, and pulled Robin across the street with me. "Look, perhaps here."

It could hardly even be called an alley, only a gap between two buildings, two feet wide at most and black as midnight. I hesitated, but then I heard a deep voice call out from around the corner, "Nine o'clock! Nine o'clock and all's well!"

The watch! Terror-stricken, I pushed Robin into the tiny passage and shoved my way in after him. Nine o'clock was the time all decent citizens should be safely at home. We could not afford to be seen on the streets so late.

We stumbled forward, brushing the walls with our shoulders. Robin stopped, and I bumped into him.

"A dead end," he whispered.

"Then we'll stay here," I whispered back. As good a place as any. I sat down with my back against a wall. Robin settled beside me.

"Rosalind?" he said after a few minutes.

"Aye."

"I'm hungry."

How could he think of his stomach? Mine roiled and twisted like a knot of snakes.

"In the morning, Robin. I'll find thee some bread in the morning."

After a time Robin's slow, deep breathing told me that he slept. I shifted to put my arm around his shoulders, and without waking he turned and nestled into me so that his head rested on my lap. His warmth was a comfort against the damp chill of the stone wall at my back.

I was at least as tired as he was; we'd walked so far that day, eager to reach London. Then there had been that panicked run through the streets. And we'd not eaten since noon. I'd thought there would be food for us at the Eastfields. I'd thought there would be safety.

My eyes drifted shut, then snapped open again with a prickle of fear.

I'd crawled into this alley like a wounded animal going to earth in a cave, but there were still sounds from the city outside drifting into our dark refuge—laughter, a snatch of drunken song, a belated cart thumping its wooden wheels along the cobblestones. Who could be abroad so late and what were they doing? At any moment, I felt, something could invade our hiding place—the watch, an apprentice with strange, pale eyes. Or the men who'd arrested the Eastfields, somehow hunting us down . . .

How had the Eastfields been betrayed? Had they been known as friends of our father? Or had he—I flinched from the thought, but it would not be denied—had he spoken their names to an interrogator in prison? He would not willingly have betrayed them, but the queen's agents had ways of forcing a man's tongue. He may have had no choice.

Just as he'd had no choice the night he'd allowed Sheriff Chapman, along with the men he had pressed into service, into our house.

None of them had seen me. Before my father had stepped away from the door, I'd retreated silently into the garden, where Robin had been dawdling, throwing stones at the crows. He and I had slipped out the back gate and had hidden near the river.

What was happening in our house was as present to my mind as if I'd been there watching. Huddled silent in the bushes with my brother, crushing sprigs of rosemary in my hands, I imagined men I'd known since childhood tearing the covers off the beds, dumping out chests, raking through the ashes in the fireplace. Was it Hugh

Forrester, the father of Robin's friend Hal, who pried up the loose board near the hearth and found the silver chalice and patten hidden underneath? Was it Adam Chandler, who'd given me sweet plums and gingerbread when I was a little girl, who discovered the hidden closet upstairs, built alongside the chimney, just large enough to hold a man?

It had been empty, thankfully. That was the only touch of mercy about the whole business. The chalice and the patten to hold the wine and bread of the Mass were enough to prove that we were Catholics, but the empty closet did not prove that we harbored priests.

We had done so, of course. Ten that I could remember. Each had stayed with us a few days in secret and then moved on to other towns to say Mass and hear confession and lift the weight of sin from faithful souls. All those things that the laws of England now made crimes, and those who did them traitors. Traitors whose heads could be set over London Bridge.

Robin and I had stayed hidden until dark had truly fallen. Then we'd dared to creep out and make our way back into our own house.

It would have been too dangerous to light a candle. We'd groped over furniture that had been overturned or shoved into unfamiliar places. My hands were shaking as

I tried to gather up the few things I could tell, by their feel, might be useful or valuable. Father kept his strong-box safely hidden in his bedroom and the key, of course, was with him. But an axe did the work as well. The crack as the metal blade bit deep into the wood made my heart leap up into my mouth as I knelt, stuffing handfuls of clinking coins into my purse. Somewhere outside, a dog barked. I told Robin we could risk no more time. We must go.

We'd walked all that night, slept the next day in a hedge, and reached the Eyres the following morning. They had fed and comforted us as best they could and sent us on our way, nearly two weary weeks of walking to reach London and the Eastfields and a new place to call home.

The city had grown silent. No more late revelers or tradesmen's carts hurrying home. The sound of running feet made my heart thump, but they passed our cavelike alley without even slowing down.

I remembered my father, in the sunlit garden, making me repeat my lesson in flight and refuge. The Masons, the Eyres, the Eastfields. Then he'd reached out and suddenly taken me in his arms, all but crushing me.

"God keep thee safe, Rosalind," he'd whispered into my hair. "And thy brother. God watch over thee."

But there was no such thing as safety. And now the

money that I had meant to help my father—to pay the fees for his food and drink and for a private cell and a bed, to keep the irons off his feet and hands—that money was gone.

"I'm sorry, Father," I whispered. "I did my best. I truly did."

The emptiness of waiting for an answer that could not come made me weep again for a while.

But at last my body's exhaustion had its say and I could not keep my eyes open any longer, despite the fear that crept in and curled next to me, so that the three of us slept huddled together, my brother and myself and my dread of what might be waiting for us in the dark.

When I woke in the morning, Robin was gone.

I found myself lying on my side, my head resting on one arm. I sat up with a panicked gasp. It was late, the sun well risen, the bright morning light finding its way even into this narrow passage. How could I have slept so long? And where was Robin? How would I face my father if something had happened to my brother?

Then there was a patter of feet on the cobblestones and Robin appeared, slipping around the mouth of the tiny alley. He grinned to see me awake. In one hand he held a loaf of brown bread.

"Robin!" I all but shrieked, forgetting that the owners of the houses on either side might hear and be less than pleased to find two vagabonds on their property. "Where hast *been*? Do not leave me like that. I thought—"

Robin's smile vanished, and he sat down beside me with a thump, ripping a chunk of bread off the loaf. "I told thee I was hungry," he muttered around a bite.

I found that I was, too. I reached over and tore off a piece of the bread for myself—coarse and brown and burnt on the bottom, but still fresh and warm. After swallowing several bites, I felt I could forgive Robin for the fright he'd dealt me.

"'Tis good," I said, and he looked a bit mollified. "How much didst pay for it?" I made up my mind I would not scold him even if he'd been cheated.

"Little."

"No, how much? We must be careful of our money."

Robin slid a sidelong glance at me, and I lowered the last bite of bread from my mouth. "Robin?"

"He had so much, Rosalind," Robin said in a wheedling tone. "Dozens of loaves all laid out. He'll hardly notice the loss. And he was fat, he could not run—"

"Thou *stolst* this?"

"But it was—"

"Robert Archer!" I was on my feet, furious. "*Stealing!* Hast no pride? Hast no *sense*? What if the baker had caught thee?"

Robin stood up as well, his cheeks flushing red. "But we needed—"

"I care not! Robin, for shame. What will our father say when he hears of this? That he has a thief for a son?"

Robin opened his mouth to argue, then shut it again and stared at the ground, a crust of the stolen bread still gripped in his fist.

"Come," I insisted, and seized him by the arm, pulling him after me out into the street. I made him show me the baker's store, and would have marched him up to the counter to apologize. But then I hesitated.

And if the baker would not be satisfied with an apology and payment? If he seized Robin and handed him over to the law? We could not risk it.

"Give me a penny," I whispered in his ear. Shamefaced, he dug into his purse and handed me a silver coin. "And stay out of sight," I told him, and made my way up to the baker's window. As I waited for my turn, I looked on loaves and rolls, tarts and gingerbread, and had a moment's sympathy for Robin as the smells of yeast and flour and honey and ginger wafted up to my nose.

"Aye, lass, what dost need?"

The baker who asked me the question was plump and redfaced, older than my father. No, he would not have been able to chase Robin far.

"Nothing," I said. "Only—a debt I have to you." And when he looked at me, puzzled, I dropped the coin into his outstretched hand.

"What's this?" he questioned, but I was already backing away. "Adam! Ask her—"

A hand was laid on my shoulder. Turning my head, I saw dark hair and a doublet of faded blue.

Even in the moment when I discerned brown eyes, not pale gray ones, I had already wrenched myself free. It was not the same man. My eyes saw it, my mind acknowledged it, but fear, senseless and strong, leaped up inside me. I pushed my way blindly into the people around me and ran when I could get free. My bruised shoulder throbbed, my heart thumped painfully, and Robin looked alarmed when I reached him.

"Rosalind? Art—"

"We are not thieves, Robin!" I told him sharply. My breath was ragged, and my words came out uneven. "We'll not let them make us so."

For a moment I thought Robin would argue, but he only nodded, and looked at me with concern.

"Art well? Rosalind?"

"Aye, of course." I twisted to look behind, to make sure the baker's apprentice had not followed.

"Will we go to see Father now?"

"Aye—" But I flinched and bit back a cry as I caught sight of a tall, dark-haired man crossing the street. It wasn't him. Of course it wasn't him. This man was laughing and held a little child by the hand. It wasn't him and yet . . .

How could we find our father in this terrible city? We might have to cross half of London to reach Newgate Prison. We would have to ask the way. *Why dost wander the streets alone, speaking to men, shameless. . . .*

All these strangers, all around me, and any of them might harbor theft or murder or worse in his heart. It was not safe. I was not safe. This was no place for Rosalind Archer, a wealthy merchant's daughter.

But I had nowhere else to go. Tears were threatening again. I pressed my trembling hands against my face. If only I had somewhere to hide, some corner like the alley we'd slept in, some cave I could crawl into.

Robin tugged at my arm. "Rosalind!" he hissed. "Art ill? People are looking."

Well enough for Robin. Oh, he was in danger, too. He might be robbed, or hurt, or taken by the law. But at least he did not have to fear what I did. He was a boy. No one would . . .

He was a boy.

I took my hands away from my face, trying to breathe slowly and steadily, and rubbed the cloth of my skirt between my fingers. It was a light worsted, soft and fine and red as wine in a clear glass, held up to the light.

My father had been a wool merchant. When our lives had still been our own, I had loved to go into his warehouse and see the rolls of cloth stacked on shelves to the ceiling. There were plenty of the sturdy, serviceable russets and browns, but I loved the colors best—butter yellow, cornflower blue, the fresh green of new grass. Sometimes, secretly, I wished for something finer, for glossy silk, fine sarcenet, or soft, heavy velvet. I imagined myself in an embroidered petticoat from Flanders, perfumed gloves of Spanish leather, a skirt of Indian calico. But I was a merchant's daughter, not a court lady, and so I had to content myself with good English wool.

It had taken me most of last winter to make the gown I was wearing now. The sleeves were long and elegant and turned back at the cuffs to show a lining of yellow linen; the skirt gathered at the waist to sweep out to my feet. The bodice was snug and stiffened with whalebone, cut low to display my best embroidered smock. The deep red flattered my skin and brought out the warm chestnut shades in my hair.

I had always been short and thin, hardly taller than Robin, though he was so much younger. A sprite, a feather, my father called me, liable to blow away in a breeze. Bone thin and scrawny, I thought to myself, with a figure that, at a quick glance, no one could tell from my brother's.

But in this gown, I felt different. I felt womanly, almost beautiful.

At his first sight of me, Father had scowled until I thought I'd somehow displeased him. Then he had smiled.

"I must look about me for a husband for thee," he'd said, and I'd blushed as red as my new gown.

But it was perilous to let my mind go back to a time when I'd been cherished and protected and sheltered. That was not my life anymore. Now I needed to devise a way for us to survive in London. That could not be, unless I could walk the streets in safety. And at the same time, find a place where Rosalind Archer might hide and never be found.

An hour or so later, I was standing in another narrow gap between two houses. I'd sent Robin to guard the mouth of the alley, where it opened out onto the street, and given him strict instructions to turn his back.

The draper whose shop we'd visited had not seemed suspicious or even interested when I'd told him I'd been sent to buy new clothing for my brother, who was just my height. Now I had breeches of thin brown wool and thick stockings that sagged at the knees and ankles, no matter how tightly I tried to fasten the garters. My own shoes, I thought, were no different from something a boy might wear. Over a plain linen shirt I pulled on a doublet of coarse russet kersey. It was not a wool my father would have allowed in his warehouse, and it was rough and harsh against my skin. I had ripped my old petticoat into strips and wrapped them tightly around my small breasts.

Now I pulled my hair loose from its pins and gathered it together at the back of my neck. I stood for a long moment with Robin's knife in my other hand.

It was a crime I intended to commit, and a sin. I knew that well enough. And soon I would stand once more before my father; what would he say to see his only daughter looking like this?

But as for crime, was I not already a criminal? And as for sin, I could only hope for forgiveness, since I had no other choice. That was something my father would understand.

I set my teeth, closed my eyes, and sawed with my knife at the thick hank of hair until it was cut through. Then I dropped it to the ground. Let it lie there. Like my old life and even my old name, it was no part of me any longer.

I picked up a flat, limp woolen cap, pulled it well down over my ears, and with my arms full of my old clothes, walked back toward the mouth of the alley to meet Robin. When I tapped him on the shoulder, he spun around, and his eyes widened until I thought they'd jump out of his head. "Rosalind," he whispered, "thou lookst—"

"Peace!" I hissed at him. "Dost want someone to hear?" I could hardly count up all the laws we were breaking at the moment, and we had no need to call attention to ourselves. "Thou'lt have to call me something else," I told Robin. "Call me—" Names tumbled through my mind. "Call me Richard." A plain, simple, commonplace name, unremarkable. No one would think twice about it, if the saints smiled upon us.

As we walked, I shivered and hugged my armful of clothing tightly. How strange it felt not to have the drag of heavy skirts behind me at each step, the tug of cloth at my waist. My head, relieved of the weight of my hair, seemed light enough to float off into the sky. I was as bare, as vulnerable, as a coney in the midst of a shorn field, with no cover from the dogs or the hunter's bow.

Surely every eye would be on me, on my legs, bare except for the thin layer of stockings, on the white skin at the back of my neck. Surely they would be able to tell, the instant they looked at me, that I was an illusion, a lie walking on two legs.

But then, hadn't I been that all my life?

When we left the second draper's shop, we were richer by the price of a red bodice and skirt, an embroidered smock, a pair of fine knit stockings, and Robin's green doublet. We bought him a simpler one of shabby blue kersey to replace it, which still left our purse some few shillings heavier.

It was not wealth, nothing compared to what had been stolen from us yesterday. But it would buy bread for a few days at least. Perhaps by the end of that time we would have found some work we could do, something simple but honest, enough to keep us from starvation.

Robin tugged impatiently at the neck of his new doublet. "Can we go *now* to see Father?" he demanded, as if I had been delaying us on purpose. When I nodded, he set off eagerly along the street. "Wait!" I called after him. "We must ask—"

At that moment, a man came tearing around the corner at a dead run and knocked us both sprawling.

chapter three
august 1592

I found myself flat on the cobblestones with a man's full
weight on top of me and a frantic voice cursing in my ear:
"God's blood, bones, body, and fingernails!" If I had not
had all the air crushed out of my lungs by the collision, I
would have been shocked breathless at such blasphemy. A
rapier in its scabbard rapped me over the shin as the
stranger clambered to his feet.

"There are a great many corners in this fair city. Did
you have to hide behind that one?" he demanded angrily.
"No time now, get up, get up!" He hooked a hand in
Robin's collar and hauled him roughly to his feet. I
scrambled upright as quickly as I could, to avoid such
treatment myself, and prepared to tell this man just what
I thought of someone who tore blindly around the city
and blamed innocent strangers for standing in his way.

But I could only stare, baffled, as the lunatic transformed

himself in an instant. Losing all trace of haste or urgency, he leaned indolently against a nearby wall. I jumped back as he drew a dagger from a sheath at his belt, but he only used it to trim his fingernails, humming an idle tune. If I hadn't known better, I would have thought he'd been standing there all day.

So he must have looked to the man who came running around the same corner a moment later. Robin dodged to avoid being flattened a second time. "Master Marlowe," the pursuer wheezed. He was red faced and panting for breath. "I—I accuse you—"

"Constable Nicholls!" the madman said affably, with a bright smile, as though the meeting were a delightful and unexpected pleasure. "Some miscreant, some caitiff, some thief or brawler has disturbed the peace? It comforts my soul to know that you are protecting us with such diligence. Let me commend you for it."

The constable had gotten his breath back, but he still stuttered with rage. "'Tis *you*, sir, have broken the peace. 'Tis *you* who have been brawling in the streets—who have disregarded the dignity of my office—who have, sir, thrown *turnips*, sir. . . ." He seemed about to burst into tears.

Master Marlowe sheathed his dagger and drew himself up in affronted amazement. "*I*, sir? Turnips, sir? And when, pray, was I guilty of all this?"

Constable Nicholls was redder than ever. "Just now, sir, you know it well. Mine own eyes saw you, not one minute since!"

"Impossible," Master Marlowe said airily, with a wave of his hand. "Your eyes have imposed upon you. Since the bells last struck the hour I have been here, waiting for a friend who promised to meet me. But do not take my word for it. Ask these two boys; they will tell you."

The constable turned to us, all but breathing fire. I felt as if a bite of apple had lodged itself in my throat, and I opened and closed my lips in helpless silence. Why should I put the sin of a lie in my mouth for this man, who had done nothing but knock me down and curse at me? But if he were indeed guilty of a crime, there would be a trial, and Robin and I would be wanted as witnesses—all of which would mean more attention from the law than we were well able to stand.

"Indeed, sir, he has been here since the bells rang," I said as sincerely as I could. Robin nodded eagerly to confirm it.

Constable Nicholls scowled at us, glared at Master Marlowe, and turned on his heel to stalk furiously away. Master Marlowe watched him out of sight and then clapped his hands and leaned back against the wall to laugh.

"Oh, excellent," he said with a sigh when the fit had ceased. "Did you mark his face? Well done. I am indebted to you both."

Now that I had leisure to observe him more closely, I could see that he was a young man, not tall, with brown hair rumpled from his run through the streets, and a neatly trimmed beard just tracing the line of his jaw. He must be rich, I thought, for his doublet was black velvet, slashed all over to show a lining of flame-orange taffeta, with tiny gilt buttons down the front and sleeves. And there was also the rapier that had caught me so sharply over the shin. A gentleman, no doubt. But why should a gentleman be running like a pickpocket from a London constable?

He chuckled again and rubbed his hands together. He wore no rings, and his long, thin fingers were mottled all over with black stains. "What service can I do to repay you?" he asked.

His smile was friendly enough, but I did not care to be drawn into conversation with a madman. "I thank you, sir, nothing." I remembered in time to dip my head rather than bend my knee in a curtsey. "Unless—" Well, we must ask the way of someone. "Can you tell us how to find Newgate Prison?"

Master Marlowe's eyebrows went up. "Newgate? Now

there's an odd thing. Most folk in this city try as hard as they can to stay clear of such a place. And you would seek it?"

"Our father's there," Robin said.

"For debt," I added quickly, and glared at Robin. We had no need to explain ourselves to this man. Why must he offer information that had not been asked for?

"Truly?" Although Master Marlowe's voice was easy, hardly interested, his eyes were narrow and alert. "And you've come from the country to visit him? You've never been in London before; 'tis easy enough to see that. Have you money?" His gaze lingered a little on my poor, patched clothing and Robin's shabby new doublet. "There's a fee to visit a prisoner."

My dismay must have shown plain on my face. "But— our own father," I protested stupidly. Surely the warden of the prison would not keep two children from seeing their father.

Master Marlowe snorted. "You're a fine pair of innocents to be wandering around the city. Have you even a place to sleep tonight? Or did you think that food and beds were free for the asking in London?"

"We had money," I said stiffly. How dare he call us fools, when he would have been in prison this moment but for us? "But it was stolen."

"No doubt. Every pickpocket on the bridge must have

had his eye on two such country coneys. Well, then. I suppose it would weigh on my conscience to abandon you. If the law does not take you in for vagabonds, there will be nothing left of you by tomorrow. Perhaps . . ." He looked at me thoughtfully and nodded. "Yes, indeed. And thou." He turned abruptly to Robin. "Canst turn a cartwheel?"

He had been talking so reasonably, I had almost forgotten that he had lost his wits. But this was too much. Was this city entirely composed of thieves, brutes, and madmen? "Sir, I thank you." Although, in truth, what had he done that I should thank him? He had not even given us the directions I'd asked for. "Good day to you."

"No, no, have patience a moment." He reached out a hand to catch at my sleeve. "There's reason in my madness, I promise you both. And you've nowhere to go, so why not humor me awhile? Go on, lad, show me."

Ridiculous. This was no time to be turning tumbling tricks in the streets of London. "Come, Robin," I started to say, but my little brother was not likely to lose a chance to show off his skills. Ever since he'd first seen a company of players, he had been mad for such foolishness. Now he turned a neat cartwheel, his heels flashing over his head, apparently to Master Marlowe's satisfaction.

"Well enough," he said, and seemed to make up his mind. "I know of a place that's looking for a new apprentice, perhaps two. It would mean beds and food if they'll take you in. Will you come and try your luck? Do not, pray, just gape at me. I've no time for it."

I swallowed down my astonishment. "Sir, this is—too much kindness. But what kind of work—?"

"Come, then, hurry. Move your legs!" And he was walking briskly away. Robin and I had to scurry not to be left behind. "I'm late as it is, and Henslowe will have my head if I interrupt. You'll see, soon enough."

There was something helpless in the way we both scrambled after Master Marlowe, as if he had caught us on a line, hooked us like fish in a river. Newgate Prison, with our father inside, seemed to be drifting downstream, farther and farther away.

And yet, if it were true, what this strange, abrupt, bewildering man had half promised—penniless as we now were, we could not afford to give up a chance of food and lodging. But what kind of work would involve cartwheels and acrobat's tricks? A gentleman dressed like this one was surely no tumbler, performing at the fairs.

"Is't safe, Ros—" Robin turned my name into a strangled cough as I glared at him. "Richard?"

Safe? Was anything at all in this city—in this kingdom—safe for either one of us? "I know not," I admitted in an undertone to Robin. "Be watchful."

Following Master Marlowe, we ducked under an arched gateway in an old wall. For an instant fear clutched at my throat as its shadow fell over me, and I was back in that dark, narrow, deserted street, facing the last man I'd trusted to guide me through London. Was this another ruse? Had he seen through my cropped hair, my boy's clothes? I'd hardly be lucky enough to escape twice—

But it wasn't an alley or a lonely corner on the other side of the gate; it was a flight of stone stairs leading down to the river. Master Marlowe, already at the bottom, waved a hand for a wherry, and the little boat came bobbing up to the narrow dock. "Come, boys, mind yourselves," Master Marlowe called as Robin and I hurried down after him and clambered unsteadily in. "The Rose, and quickly," he told the boatman, handing him his fare.

I might have taken the opportunity to question Master Marlowe further about the work he'd mentioned, but the thick, oily stench of the river and the rocking of the little boat made me feel it was wisest to sit very still on the cushioned bench, with my teeth clenched and my mouth shut tight. The boatman's oars knocked into bits of floating refuse: a limp fish, a log, something that might have been a dead pig and that made even Master Marlowe grimace as it nudged the hull and spun gently away into the current.

To my right London Bridge stretched over the Thames. Could it truly have been just yesterday that Robin and I walked over its span? I sat facing backward and could see the city itself, houses crowded close to the riverbank, docks bristling into the water. Little wherries like ours and large ships with masts and sails clustered around the docks, waiting for owners or customers. And looming over everything was the bulk of St. Paul's Cathedral, higher than any other building, a square stone pile, severe and strong.

Master Marlowe, it seemed, had seen this sight too often to be impressed, or perhaps he had other things on his mind. He did not turn to look, but sat facing forward, frowning. "Canst go no faster?" he demanded.

"God sets the wind and the current and the tide, master," the boatman grunted, not altering the steady sweep of his oars. Master Marlowe sighed. And the instant the boat touched the dock on the south side of the Thames, he was up, calling to Robin and me to stir ourselves and follow.

We trailed him along the riverbank a little way, and down another narrow street, and then we saw our destination.

It was a tall building, three entire stories, the walls plastered a fresh, clean white. And it was round. It looked strange, and a bit unearthly, like something that might

spring up overnight from a fairy ring. A flag was flutter-
ing atop, snapping bright orange against the sky.

A man passing by stopped Master Marlowe with a
touch on his shoulder. "Good day to you, and what's the
play to be this afternoon?" he asked.

"*Faustus*," Master Marlowe answered briefly.

Robin turned to me with widened eyes. "'Tis a *playhouse!*" he whispered, awestruck and delighted.

We had fallen a bit behind Master Marlowe, and now I
snatched at Robin's arm to keep him back. Master
Marlowe thought we might find work at a playhouse? A
blush scorched my cheeks at the thought. To watch a play
was one thing, but everyone knew players were shameless
and immodest. How could they be otherwise, lying for
their living, displaying vice and sin, murder and adultery,
on the stage for all to see?

My breeches and doublet and chopped-off hair might
have saved me from one kind of peril, but here was another
opening up like a pit at my feet. I would not allow this disgrace to overtake us either. We might be lost and penniless,
far from home, alone, but we had not sunk so far. We would
not sweep floors in a brothel, or carry filth from privies to
the river, and we would not work in a playhouse.

"Let be!" Robin protested, trying to twist his arm free
from my grasp.

"No!" I hissed at him. I prepared to raise my voice, to thank Master Marlowe for his pains and tell him we would go no farther.

But Robin winced as I tightened my grip, and I remembered belatedly how the man with the squint had twisted his arm behind him. I let go with a rush of shame. "I'm sorry, Robin. Come now—"

Robin's jaw was tight and stubborn. "No. I want to see," he insisted. And before I could stop him, he had darted after Master Marlowe, who'd turned back to see why we delayed.

I might have known that Robin would not be dissuaded. Two summers ago traveling players had come to our village and set up stage in the inn yard. I had eaten nuts and laughed at the clown and cheered the swordfight and gone home well satisfied. But Robin—Robin had begged and pleaded until our father had taken him back to see the play a second time and then a third. Each time he'd stood without moving, his eyes locked on the stage, so tightly drawn with excitement he seemed to vibrate like a plucked lute string.

After that Robin began to practice his tumbling tricks by the riverbank. When the other boys talked of running away to serve on a privateer and seize ships of Spanish gold, Robin talked of running away to London to join a company of players.

It was all nonsense, of course. Robin would no more cut capers on a stage than his friend Hal would ship out as a sailor for Sir Francis Drake. Robin would be a wool merchant when he grew to be a man, and in the meantime our father had chuckled indulgently and promised to take him to London one day to see real players.

But now Robin dashed after Master Marlowe, his face alight with eagerness, as if he had forgotten why we were here, and why all things were different now, and why he would never be a merchant like our father. The two of them disappeared inside the playhouse doors. And I could only follow them into that den of wickedness, or be left behind alone.

Inside the playhouse I found myself in a broad, bare yard. Nutshells, left from the last performance, crunched under my feet. All around us rose the circle of the galleries, three rings of them, one on top of the other. The stage at the far end had a roof supported by pillars, all of it painted blue and red and green and gold, so bright in the sunlight that tears stung my eyes.

In the yard below the stage, two men were engaged in a desperate swordfight. Master Marlowe, with Robin already at his side, ignored them and waved a hand at a boy in a long gown of red brocade who sat on the edge of the stage, swinging his feet and crunching an apple.

Behind him, like something out of a painting of hell, the head of a dragon reared up, its open mouth wide enough for a man to stand up between the rows of sharp teeth.

"Harry!" Master Marlowe shouted across the yard. "Where's Henslowe?"

The boy swallowed the last bite of his apple and tossed the core carelessly across the yard. "Backstage," he answered lazily.

"Go fetch him for me." The boy only yawned. "Do it, or I'll tell the tireman thou wast eating in that gown!" Master Marlowe threatened. "He'll nail thine ears to a post and slice them off. Go!"

The boy Harry got gracefully to his feet, smoothed his skirts, and sauntered off through a door at the back of the stage. "Impudent dog," Master Marlowe grumbled. "I'll have his ears off myself."

I caught up with the two of them and scowled at Robin, but he paid me no heed, and I knew that short of laying hands on him and dragging him across the yard, I could not move him. Ignoring me, Robin turned to Master Marlowe. "Are you a player, sir?"

Master Marlowe looked down at him, almost in surprise, as if he'd forgotten we had speech, or were more than inanimate blocks trailing him through London. "A player? No, that I am not."

I was bewildered again, and Robin's face fell.

"No, boy, I am not a mere speaker of another man's words," Master Marlowe went on. He began to walk toward the stage, maneuvering easily around the two duelists. "I am much more than that." One of the swordsmen lunged, and his blade seemed to sink deep into his opponent's chest. The victim gasped, moaned, and doubled over to fall dramatically at my feet, where he looked up at me and winked. I had to step over him to keep up with Master Marlowe, who had reached the stage and climbed easily up on it. He swept his arm in a grand gesture, just as a dark-haired, bearded, harassed-looking man opened a door in the back wall. "In fact, I am the foundation on which the entire Rose playhouse rests. Is't not true, Henslowe?"

"You are the plague of my life, Christopher, is what you are," Master Henslowe grumbled. "I've a performance to put on, and you must come hanging about—and what is *this* doing here?" he bellowed, slapping the dragon's head with one hand.

A man popped out of the dragon's mouth, startling me so badly that I jumped. "Only shifting some things backstage, master," he explained mildly.

"Well, get on with it," Master Henslowe said irritably, and the man disappeared back into the dragon's gullet. "And you, Kit, what is't you need? Be quick."

"Ungrateful wretch." Master Marlowe sighed, wounded and reproachful. "When see what a gift I've brought you. Come up here, boy." He reached a hand down to Robin, who took it and was hauled easily up onto the stage. "Show him what you did for me."

Robin obediently flipped into a cartwheel, and then turned a row of somersaults as I stood fuming helplessly in the yard below. When a trapdoor opened suddenly in the center of the stage, Robin nearly tumbled in. A thin, sandy-haired man in a patchwork doublet of green and yellow silk popped his head up through the hole.

"Master Henslowe," this man said, paying Robin no heed, "there's a—"

"Speak to the bookkeeper," Henslowe interrupted him, and the man ducked down again like a rabbit into its hole. "Well, what else, boy?"

Robin did his best trick, a handstand. He was not very good at this yet, and his legs wavered unsteadily in the air. Henslowe frowned.

"You need another boy for that last scene, now that Ned has left you for the Queen's Men," Master Marlowe said persuasively. "He'll not have to do much, just cut capers and run about."

"Well enough, I suppose," Henslowe said, just as Robin fell over with a thump.

Robin sat up, rubbing an elbow. "I can do it better," he said quickly, fervently. "Pardon, masters, let me try again."

I was startled to see Henslowe chuckle a little. "No need, lad. Bring him around after the performance, Kit, and we'll find him a place to stay."

Robin's smile nearly split his face from ear to ear. But I was not smiling.

My brother was no vagabond player. How could I let him shame our family like this?

But how could I stop him? He would not listen to a thing I said. To argue with him or scold him now would do nothing more than draw attention to myself. And dressed as I was, attention was something I could ill afford.

"And what's this, another?" Master Henslowe asked, turning his eye on me.

I choked out a horrified denial, which neither of them heard, for Master Marlowe was already talking.

"Now this, Henslowe, you *will* thank me for. Come up here, boy." I obeyed, thinking that they would hear me better if I stood on their own level. "Look now," Master Marlowe continued, and before I could prevent it, he had snatched off my hat. "You see? Zenocrate or Isabel. Harry is getting too old to play the girls' parts. Soon we'll have a Helen with a beard on her chin."

"But masters—," I objected.

They ignored me. "He's too old," Henslowe said, shaking his head. "Hast ever played a part before, lad?"

"No, sir," I said emphatically. "And to say truth—"

"Henslowe, *look* at that face," Master Marlowe countered impatiently. "He'll hardly have to act, he looks so much a girl."

"I am no player!" I almost shouted it. I could have added more, that I was decent and God-fearing and mindful of my family's reputation even if my brother was not. But Master Marlowe's last words had frightened me so badly that, when the two men turned to me in surprise, I only ducked my head to look down at the boards of the stage.

"I pray you pardon me," I mumbled. "I cannot play a part."

My heart beat quick as a bird's against my ribs. If they kept looking at me so, they were sure to guess. Master Marlowe had come too close already.

"Come, lad, 'tis nothing but nerves," Master Marlowe said heartily. I only shook my head, not looking up. Silence was surely the best way to dissuade them.

"Well, Kit, if he does not wish it, that's all there is," Henslowe said after a moment.

Master Marlowe looked reproachfully at me. "I've

done my best for thee," he said in a low voice. "Wilt not try thy hand?"

I retrieved my hat from him and pulled it back on. With the relief of having my head covered and my face shadowed again, I could even feel a twinge of remorse. I supposed, by his lights, Master Marlowe had truly tried to do me a kindness. Probably he had no idea how decent people regarded a playhouse. He had not meant to insult me with the offer. I must have seemed churlish and ungrateful to him.

"Master, I thank you, truly," I said, without looking up. "But I cannot. I've reasons for it." And that was as much as I could tell him.

"But the other, he will do," Henslowe was saying. "What's thy name, lad?"

"Robin Archer, master," Robin said timidly.

"And thou wishest to be an apprentice with the Admiral's Men?"

Robin nodded, his eyes shining.

"Well, we'll take thee on trial, then. A week, to see how thou dost. Now, Kit, listen. . . ."

I looked down at the stage, wondering bleakly where I would go when this was all over. Back out into the streets again, I supposed, this time alone. And my faithless traitor of a brother was listening eagerly to the players' talk, as if he did not care a jot what became of me.

The boards of the stage were not painted brightly like the rest, but were bare wood, worn smooth by the tread of many feet. A lone sheet of paper drifted about in a slight breeze. It came to rest by my shoe, and I bent down to pick it up, smoothing it carefully. It seemed a player's part. I read a few lines at random.

Hell hath no limits, nor is circumscrib'd
In one self place, but where we are is hell,
And where hell is, there must we ever be.

I shivered and looked up at the dragon's head that gaped over the stage. Like this city, it seemed poised to swallow us up, the way prison had swallowed up my father. And this bit of paper hinted that there would be no way out.

Idle thoughts. The dragon's head was but wood and painted cloth. And the paper was nothing but a player's speech, insubstantial as air. I held it out to Master Marlowe.

"Sir, I think this may be wanted. 'Tis a player's part, for—" I squinted at the page again. "For Mephostophilis."

"Nick has been letting his part lie about?" Henslowe demanded angrily as Master Marlowe took the paper from me. "I paid for this play, damn him, and he wants to let every other company in London have it for free?"

"You did not pay so very much, as I recall," Master Marlowe said dryly. But then he looked at me more sharply. "Thou canst read this?"

"Aye," I answered. Why should he care?

Two men appeared to lay hold of the dragon's head and push it through the door at the back of the stage. A squeal from a badly tuned viol or rebec came from overhead. "Kit, get off my stage, will you?" Master Henslowe demanded. "Take our new apprentice here and watch the performance, and keep yourself, if you can, from telling him all the players are doing it wrong. Yes, I'm coming!" he shouted to someone I couldn't see. "Begone, Kit, take these two with you."

chapter four

AUGUST 1592

Master Marlowe led us off the stage and into the first row of galleries. He motioned for Robin to take a seat on one of the long wooden benches, but I hesitated.

I was no player's apprentice. There was no place for me here. But if I walked out of the playhouse now, I did not know where I would go or what I'd do. I did not even know if the three shillings and the few odd pence I had left in my purse would be enough to buy my way into Newgate Prison so I could see my father.

Master Marlowe had seated himself alongside Robin. But he paid no heed to him, frowning instead at me. "What's thy name?" he demanded.

I remembered in time what my new name was. "Richard Archer, master."

"And canst read?"

I could not imagine why it mattered so to him

whether or not I was lettered. "I can."

"Prove it." He held out to me the paper I had picked up from the stage.

I squinted at the scribbled lines and they came clear to me, although it made little sense, being only the words set down for one player to speak. Lacking the answers to questions, or the questions to answers, it was but a jumble. Still, I cleared my throat and read. "'So now, Faustus, ask me what thou wilt. Under the heavens. Within the bowels of these elements, where we are tortur'd and remain for ever.'"

Master Marlowe lifted his eyebrows. "And canst write a fair hand as well?"

"Aye, sir, I can write." Robin had studied Latin at the grammar school with the other boys, but my father had taught me at home. I should have enough knowledge of numbers that no shopkeeper could cheat me, he said, and enough of letters to write down what the household bought and spent. I had been good with my pen; I wrote a fairer hand than Robin. Master Marlowe's words brought back, with a sting of tears in my eyes, the bitter smell of ink, the honey-colored surface of the old table in the back of the warehouse, and my father's presence at my shoulder, watching as the quill in my hand scratched steadily over the paper.

"Indeed," Master Marlowe said, eyeing me as if I were a horse at market. "If 'tis true, I might have use for thee. The law will take thee up for a vagabond if thou'rt not in service, so thou mayst as well be in mine."

The word "no" sat on my tongue. I did not wish to be this man's servant, and it was not my pride that revolted at the idea. To be a servant was not grand, but it was honest.

But in truth, I was baffled, and in my confusion, even afraid. Why should Master Marlowe be so kind? He had offered twice now to save me from begging in the streets, but he hardly looked at me, leaning back on the bench, his legs stretched out before him, his eyes on the empty stage. His careless manner made it seem as if my life were a matter of indifference—he might save it or lose it, it was all the same to him.

Nevertheless, I knew I'd be a fool to throw aside this second chance. Work, food, a bed, wages even—I must take it and be grateful. "Master, I thank you," I said as humbly as I could. "God reward you for your kindness."

Master Marlowe made an impatient gesture with one hand. "'Tis not kindness. I'll take thee on trial for a week. If thou canst do the work I need, I'll feed and clothe thee. If not, I'll not keep thee. And by this light, do not start a rumor that I have a conscience. My reputation would never survive it."

The porter had opened the doors and people were starting to stream into the playhouse as I sat down on the bench by the side of my new master. Apprentices and servants and townspeople mindful of economy pushed forward to stand close to the stage, while the more prosperous filled up the galleries. I stared in astonishment as a man with skin the color of coal found a seat in the galleries near to us. An elegant woman in a long black cloak and a silk mask, attended by a gentle-man in deep red satin, climbed to the rooms over the stage and sat there at her ease, as if she were uncon-scious that all eyes were upon her. In the little room next to her, the musicians were practicing. Sweet scraps of tunes from a lute and a viol drifted out into the play-house, and a man put a hautboy to his lips and blew a silvery scattering of notes, like raindrops tossed by the wind, over the heads of the crowd.

"Master Marlowe?" Robin asked shyly.

"What?"

"If you are not a player, sir, what is't you do here?"

"Hast not guessed? I am a playmaker. 'Tis my play they are about to perform. And very poorly, too, no doubt."

So that was why he had claimed to be the foundation of the playhouse. The players would have no words to speak but for him.

"Ho there!" Master Marlowe's attention had been caught by someone just entering the playhouse. He waved a hand. "Tom! Tom Watson!"

The man who came to put his elbows on the railing of our gallery was taller than Master Marlowe by a handspan, handsome and well made. His crisp, white ruff set off a thin, dark face. "Ah, Kit, I thought I'd find you here," he said.

"Where else? Are you not teaching this day?"

"The brat is sick, or says he is," Master Watson answered, and he cast his eye upon Robin and myself. "And who are these?"

"This one I plan to try for a servant," Master Marlowe said. "And the other will be an apprentice at the Rose."

"An apprentice here?" Master Watson turned his attention to Robin. "Brave heart. Dost truly dare to appear in such a play as this?"

"Aye, I think so," Robin said uncertainly. "If I have the skill." He glanced at Master Marlowe to see if this was the right answer.

"Has no one told thee? Shame, Kit, you should have warned him. Dost know, boy, that there is a scene in this play where the devil himself is summoned?"

"Enough, Tom, 'tis foolishness," Master Marlowe objected.

His friend ignored him. "And knowst that often the players have made a count of who is on stage when the devil is called—and they find one man too many?" His voice dropped dramatically. "Pray, who dost think that extra man might be?"

"Go to," Master Marlowe snapped. "It only proves that no player has the wit to count above five. Mind you, if the devil himself were to appear on the stage, I would not object. No doubt he could play the part better than Nick."

I stifled a gasp of alarm at such careless talk, and Robin looked around as if afraid that the devil might take Master Marlowe at his word. Master Watson only laughed.

"I'll find a seat, then, for they're about to start. Kit, I must speak a word with you—"

"Not just now," Master Marlowe said quietly, and Master Watson moved off as the trumpet sounded and the play began.

A scholar in a long, black robe sat on the stage, poring over his books. I shuddered as he tossed aside philosophy, medicine, law, and even religion, to seize on black magic as the only study fit for a wise man.

Master Marlowe was quiet through the early scenes, only once or twice hissing through his teeth and muttering, "Too fast, too fast." But when the scholar chalked symbols on the floor and chanted Latin and conjured spirits, he fell silent, as did the whole audience. We all held our breath, and when a mighty figure, with black skin and horns springing from his forehead, leaped up from the trapdoor as if he'd come from the bowels of hell, everyone gasped at once, with a sound like wind in the leaves.

"'Now, Faustus, what wouldst thou have me do?'" the devil roared. A woman in the audience shrieked. Master Marlowe, with his elbows braced on his knees, dropped his forehead onto his clenched fists.

"'Sblood, *no*," I heard him groan. "Ranting, raving, mad, fantastical bombast . . ." And he didn't look up for the rest of the scene.

I could not take my eyes from the stage, where the scholar, Faustus, carelessly bargained his soul away. He repented in the end, but it was far too late. Even Master Marlowe sat quiet and attentive as small devils leaped out of the dragon's mouth I had seen earlier and capered around the stage. They were only boys, I realized, most of them Robin's age. Though the summer sky was bright overhead, the stage seemed dark, somehow, and thunder rumbled. "'My God, my God, look not so fierce on me,'" Faustus moaned. With a roar of triumph, the devil seized him and hauled him back between the dragon's teeth.

Robin was staring openmouthed at the stage. I felt myself shivering. Would the devil and Faustus really come hand in hand to take their bows? It seemed impossible. But they did, and the crowd burst into applause as Master Marlowe sat hunched over with his elbows on his knees and scowled.

He didn't stir while the playhouse emptied. At last, when the audience had all departed, he got up and, without a word to us, climbed over the gallery railing, dropped easily on the other side, vaulted up on the stage, and disappeared through the door at the back.

Robin would have followed him, but this was my first chance to speak to him alone, and I did not mean to waste it. "Robin, how couldst thou?" I demanded. "A player's apprentice? For shame!"

"'Tis not so terrible," Robin muttered sulkily, not meeting my eyes. "'Tis no crime. And what else was I to do? We've no money now."

"We could have found some other work."

"Cleaning privies? Sweeping horse dung off the streets?"

"Dost think we came to London to make thee a player? Didst think of our father at all?"

Robin's face went white and then flushed red across the cheekbones. "Aye, I did," he said coldly, and lifted his eyes to my face at last. "And thou'rt one to speak of shame. What will our father say when he sees thee?"

I felt as if he'd slapped me. Leaving me sick and stunned, he climbed over the gallery railing and followed Master Marlowe backstage.

How could he say such a thing to me? My own brother, who knew well enough what had happened—had nearly happened—yesterday. How dare he? Hot fury burned away my shock, and I leaped up and went after him. But I did not have a chance to start another argument with Robin, because a different confrontation was already taking place.

The space behind the stage seemed much too narrow to contain all the people inside it. A man with spectacles on his nose brushed past me, his arms overflowing with silk and velvet and lace. I saw the boy Harry, now in his proper clothes, perched on a ladder that led up to the chamber above the stage. The tall, dark-haired man who had played Faustus stood talking to Henslowe, idly stroking the neat triangle of a beard on his chin, while the devil himself sat on a chest and scrubbed with a damp cloth at the charcoal that covered his face.

It was the devil Master Marlowe was berating. "Nick!" the playmaker exploded just as I slipped through the door. "What do you call *that*? Bellowing, howling, bleating—are you a dog, a goat, or a cat in heat?"

The player Nick, his face now smeared half black and

half white, seemed no more than amused. "'Tis what people expect, Kit, when they look at the devil," he said in a tone of patient reason.

"Expect!" Master Marlowe spat. "Do you think the devil walks among us like *that*, horns and tail and all?" He had by now collected an audience of players, who gathered around, some frowning, some smiling in delight at a rousing scene. "Do you think the devil knows nothing of subtlety?" Master Marlowe went on. "Do you think he's never heard of craft? I tell you, if the devil were among us right now, none of you would know it. He walks like a man, looks like a man; he gets souls by whispering, not by shouting."

"Well, I could not say, Kit, not having such a close acquaintance with him as you do," Nick said easily.

The others chuckled, and the man who had been Faustus clapped. "Well played!" he called out, and bowed toward Nick.

Henslowe held up his hands. "Enough! Pray, Master Alleyn, do not encourage them. Kit, the way he plays it fills up the galleries, and that should satisfy you. It does me, at all events. Out, now, let them set the stage up for tomorrow. Rehearsal in the morning, all. Where's our new apprentice?"

Master Marlowe looked around as if he'd forgotten

that we existed. Henslowe saw us at the same moment. "Robin, is't? This is Master Cowley. Thou'lt be lodging at his home. Tomorrow thou'lt come to rehearsal, and we'll begin teaching thee what thou needst to know."

Master Cowley was a kindly looking man with a grizzled beard of black and white. Thinking back, I remembered that he had played one of Faustus's friends. "Come, lad," he said warmly to Robin. "I've two other crackropes lodged with me, so thou'lt make friends soon enough."

Aye, friends among players and other riffraff of the streets. Well enough, if he preferred it. Why should I mind?

"Come, boy," Master Marlowe said to me as he turned to go.

Robin looked at the ground, refusing to meet my eyes. But he muttered, "Farewell, Richard."

I tightened my lips and, without a word, followed my new master back across the stage, out of the playhouse, and into the streets of London.

It would not be for long. That was what I vowed to myself as I hurried behind Master Marlowe. I was on a week's trial as a servant, and Robin as an apprentice. By the end of that time, I would have found a way to change things.

I'd hardly been two hours in Master Marlowe's service;

I could not ask him for leave at this moment to find Newgate. But tomorrow, no matter what else took place, I would make my way to the prison. My father would tell me what was best to do; he would order Robin away from the playhouse. My brother might pay no heed to me, but he would be bound to obey his father's word.

By a week's end, if not sooner, this would be over. Robin would no longer be a 'prentice player and I would no longer be in service with a man who spoke as if he were on terms of close acquaintance with the devil himself.

In the meantime I kept close at Master Marlowe's heels as he led me back to London Bridge, and for the second time in two days I crossed its span. He walked rapidly north along a wide street, past the fish markets I had seen earlier, past churches and houses and taverns and store-fronts. I was nearly breathless, trying to keep pace with him.

We had walked perhaps a mile when I almost trod on a heap of greasy rags by the roadside. I nearly shrieked aloud as the rags moved and a bare, skinny arm thrust out. A face, too, appeared under a ragged cowl, but I could not tell if this were a man or a woman.

He—or she, perhaps—spoke no word. Eyes so deeply shadowed I could not tell their color only looked up at me and the outstretched hand pleaded mutely.

I hesitated. It was sinful to beg. All who could should work for a living—

But if Master Marlowe had not taken me in, or if I failed to find some other plan before the week was out, would I come to this?

"Dost pay heed, Richard?" Master Marlowe asked, turning back to see what delayed me. He frowned, but slipped a hand into his purse and tossed a silver halfpenny in the beggar's direction. She—or he?—snatched it out of the air and huddled back into the rags.

"Thou'lt need to find thy way about," was all Master Marlowe said as I caught up with him, as if the beggar were not worthy of comment. "There's the city wall, dost see?" He pointed ahead. The wall, its stones black with dirt and age, rose higher than my head, and I realized with surprise that we had crossed the city from south to north. "And Bishopsgate," Master Marlowe added. That must be the arched opening that we were rapidly approaching. "My lodgings are in Norton Folgate; 'tis a ways beyond the wall."

"Why so far, sir?" I asked, trying to put the beggar's hungry stare out of my mind. Judging from Master Marlowe's clothing, he was wealthy enough. Why did he not live in a fine house within the city itself?

"Most of us live beyond the city proper," Master

Marlowe explained. "Players and playmakers, the lot of us. The playhouses are outside the city boundaries as well. The Lord Mayor is not so fond of us as he might be." He chuckled, but there seemed to be little mirth in it. "Some say we cause riots, and some say we cause plagues, and yet they all keep coming to see the plays."

We had passed through the gate by now. I had expected green fields to begin on the other side of the wall and was startled to find little change, the houses still crowded together, the road still paved beneath my feet. "The city outgrew its old jacket many years ago," Master Marlowe said, noticing my surprise. "Not much farther now."

Master Marlowe's lodgings, when we reached them at last, were on the third floor of a bakery run by a widow, Mistress Stavesly. She came out to greet us, a tall, plain, red-haired woman, and stood dusting the flour from her hands as Master Marlowe introduced me.

"The boy will need a place to sleep," he said. "Have you a pallet you can lend me, mistress?"

"Aye, I can let you have that."

I dipped my head to her. "Thank you, mistress."

"Such manners," she said dryly. "I'll think I'm at the court next. Master Marlowe, your rent is due tomorrow, kindly remember."

"I hear and obey," Master Marlowe said, and bowed

elaborately, as if she were the queen. She snorted and went back to her kitchen.

Master Marlowe's lodging turned out to be nothing more than two rooms, each with one many-paned window. In the front room was a fireplace, a stool, and a table littered with papers and quills. On a shelf above the table there leaned some books and a lute, dusty as if untouched for many weeks. A few tankards and bowls and a spoon or two sat on another shelf. In the back room were Master Marlowe's bed and a chest for his clothes. And that seemed to be all. A poor enough living space for someone who wore velvet and carried a sword like a rich gentleman.

I stood in the front room, feeling lost and not at all sure what a playmaker's servant was supposed to do. But Master Marlowe decided the question for me. "I'm off," he announced. "Thou canst. . . ." He shrugged. "Settle thyself, I suppose." With a wave of his hand, he seemed to say that I should make myself at home. "Ah, thou'lt need to be fed, I imagine. There's bread left over from the morning. Take what thou wilt." He pointed at the windowsill, where half a loaf of bread was wrapped in a napkin to keep it from the flies. Master Marlowe disappeared into the back room. A glimpse through the doorway showed him running a comb through his hair. He brushed the dust of the street from his doublet, polished the gilt buttons carefully against his sleeve, and was off again without offering me a word of farewell.

I was not alone for long, however, before Mistress Stavesly came puffing up the stairs with a heavy straw mattress in her arms. I ran to help her drag it into the room, and we laid it out in a corner by the fireplace. Without a word beyond, "Wait thee," she departed again, and came back with a pair of rough woolen blankets under one arm. This freed her hands to carry a wooden bowl of pottage and a leather tankard of ale.

"I do not suppose he'll have thought to feed thee," she said gruffly, waving away my thanks. "Off to the alehouse again, is he?"

"I know not," I said, though my heart sank. Was *that* where he had gone? Was he a drunkard as well as a play-maker and a man who claimed to know in what shape the devil walked among us? "Have you known Master Marlowe long, mistress?"

"I know him not," she said sternly. "He pays his rent each week, and I ask no more." She looked at me, I thought, in disapproval. "What possessed him to take thee into service, I cannot imagine. But do not count on his good humor too far. He's changeable as March wind." Shaking her head, she made her way down the stairs.

Her words might be discouraging, but her pottage was

excellent, the oatmeal soft and thick, the chunks of mutton tender. And I was ravenous. Now I came to think of it, I had not eaten since Robin's stolen loaf of bread that morning, back in the time I was still Rosalind Archer.

Rosalind Archer would have eaten her dinner at a table, with a cook to prepare it and a maid to serve. There would have been, perhaps, a joint of mutton, a cut of beef, or a capon stewed and savory. And her father and brother would have been there with her. She would not have crouched on the edge of a straw pallet, leery of sitting on the only stool in case Master Marlowe would think it a presumption, scouring the pottage bowl clean with chunks of bread and stuffing them into her mouth. Embarrassed, I sat up straight, wiped my face, and finished what was left of my food in a more seemly fashion. Because I was not what I had been, it did not follow that I must be an animal. I would eat as if I'd been taught manners. My father would not be ashamed of me, if he could see me.

Or would he? I set the empty bowl and tankard down on the floor and rubbed one hand at the back of my neck. *What will our father say when he sees thee?* Had Robin been right? Would my father be shocked beyond measure at the sight of me, shameless and immodest in my breeches and doublet? Would he think I had disgraced myself to become the servant of a playmaker, a man who lied for profit? Would he condemn me for it? Would God?

I reached into my shirt and pulled a thin leather cord over my head. Attached to the cord, in a small linen bag, was my rosary.

I held the wooden beads, warm from the heat of my body, between my fingers and began to pray. "*Ave Maria, gratia plena. . . .*"

The words wrapped themselves around me, soft and comforting, like summer sunlight, like a fur-lined cloak in winter. "*Dominus tecum, benedicta tua. . . .*" I had much need of grace today. I had lied, I had abandoned the name I'd been christened with, I had entered the service of a playmaker and a blasphemer. And since I did not know where to find a priest in London, I could not even confess and have my sins lifted off my heart. But as I prayed my way around the beads, I could only trust that God would understand. And so would my father. They would know that what I'd done, I'd done so that I could survive.

I was a Catholic at heart, even if that must stay secret, just as I was a woman under my breeches and doublet. My lies were only on the surface. They did not change the deepest truths. When I had prayed all fifty-five prayers, I tucked the rosary back underneath my shirt and waited for my new master to return and tell me what he wished me to do.

Light faded from the window, and the sky outside turned gold, then rose, then purple, then black. And Master Marlowe still did not appear. At length I took off my shoes and doublet and unwrapped the bands around my breasts, gently rubbing the sore spots where the linen had chafed the tender skin. I hid the strips of cloth, along with the rosary, under the pallet and fell asleep listening for the sound of Master Marlowe's footsteps on the stairs.

chapter five
AUGUST 1592

~

I never heard Master Marlowe come in that night. But when I woke in the morning, he was lying, facedown and snoring quietly, under the blankets of his bed.

The straw pallet had not been overly comfortable. I sat up, stiff and sore, rubbed my face, stretched, and began to consider the complicated matter of getting dressed. I had slept in my shirt and breeches, for modesty, and with Master Marlowe in the next chamber, I did not dare take off the shirt to wind the linen wrappings about my breasts again. He seemed thoroughly asleep, but he might wake at any moment, and the door between the rooms was not shut fully.

In the end I pulled my doublet over my head, stuffed the strips of linen inside it, and tucked my rosary back into the bag around my neck. Then I made my way downstairs. I passed the second floor, where Mistress Stavesly slept, and the bakery, where the smell of fresh bread in the air was almost enough to chew and swallow. In the yard behind the building, I found what I had been hoping for—a privy. There, in the stinking darkness, I adjusted the wrappings to my satisfaction, then came outside, fully Richard once again.

And Richard needed to decide what to do. Master Marlowe had not looked likely to stir anytime soon, so I was obliged to set about my role as a playmaker's servant without any guidance from him. My new master, as far as I could judge from yesterday, did not seem to be a patient man. If I wanted to stay in his service for even a brief time, it would be wise to prove myself worth my keep.

There were a few wooden buckets, I noticed, in one corner of the yard. Fetching water was surely a servant's task. I found the public conduit near Bishopsgate, filled a bucket, and lugged it back, knocking the rim against my knee at every step and spilling water down into my shoe. I'd never thought much before about how heavy water was, and I felt a touch of remorse to think of the times I'd scolded Joan for her slowness when I sent her to the well.

In the lodgings once more, with Master Marlowe still snoring, I dipped my hands in the water and scrubbed my face. No soap; I would have to make do without.

What next? I looked around at the bare room and

rubbed the toe of my shoe over the gritty floorboards. The room had not been swept in weeks, surely. I went downstairs to beg a broom of Mistress Stavesly.

The big brick oven at the back of the bakery filled the shop with a heat that seemed solid, as if I'd walked into a wall. Mistress Stavesly was just sliding a batch of loaves on a long-handled wooden platter into the oven's open mouth. She wore only a sleeveless bodice over her skirts, and sweat ran down her face from under her cap. "Thou'rt starting early to work," she said in answer to my question. "Aye, take a broom and welcome. My daughter Moll can show thee. Here, Moll!" The girl who came shambling up in answer to the call was a head and more taller than I was, ghostly white from head to toe with flour. "Moll, show Richard where a broom is. She's half-witted," Mistress Stavesly explained to me. "But if thou'lt say anything twice or three times over, she'll understand."

Moll did not seem to mind the words. She only looked curiously and shyly at me from behind the tangles of dark hair that hung in her eyes.

"A broom, please?" I asked. She blinked, as if considering my outlandish request, and then brought me to a corner of the shop, where a broom of neatly trimmed twigs leaned on its bristles.

"I'm Moll," she announced abruptly.

"Aye, I know it," I answered. She was looking at me expectantly, and I realized what she wanted. "Oh, I am Richard. My thanks for the broom, Moll." She beamed as if I'd given her a shilling.

I used the broom to knock cobwebs down from the slanted ceiling and shake the spiders outside, and then began on the floor. But as I swept under the table, I paused, and glanced cautiously into the other room. Master Marlowe slept on. I set the broom against the table and looked at the papers there.

No wonder Master Marlowe had wanted a servant who could write a fair hand. The sheets scattered about were closely covered in a spiky writing that would have been hard to make out even if half the words had not been heavily scored through, blotted, or smeared. I didn't dare touch the papers; Master Marlowe might notice if they'd been rearranged. But one in particular caught my eye.

It was tucked under another page so that I could see only a corner, but it was not written in a language I had ever seen. Not English or French or Latin. Might it be Greek? Was Master Marlowe so learned? I bent closer to peer at a jumble that looked like bird tracks and worm castings. And then I remembered the symbols that the player Nick had chalked on the stage floor yesterday. That was a play, a fiction, an illusion. Was this truth? Was

Master Marlowe worse than a Protestant? Did he, like Faustus, practice black magic?

In the next room, the ropes beneath the mattress creaked. I jumped away from the table and snatched at the broom. When Master Marlowe appeared in the doorway, running both hands through his rumpled hair, I was industriously sweeping the dirt from the floor into the fireplace.

"Ah, Richard," he said, yawning fit to crack his jaw and squinting as though the light hurt his eyes. He was still wearing his hose but nothing else. I fastened my eyes on the floor. "Hard at work, I see. Fetch some water, then."

"There, sir." Without looking up, I pointed at the bucket in the corner.

"Thou mayst be worth thy keep after all," Master Marlowe said, as if surprised. "Fill up that basin, so I can wash."

I filled the wooden bowl with water, found soap and linen towels where he told me to look for them, and kept my eyes studiously elsewhere as he knelt on the floor of his bedroom to scrub his face and hands clean and run handfuls of water through his hair. Shaking his wet head like a dog, Master Marlowe got to his feet and looked at me curiously. "What, boy, art ill? Thou'rt red as a poppy."

I dreaded his sharp eyes, but I could not keep the heat

back from my cheeks. "Only a bit warm, sir," I said feebly. This was a complication I had not thought of when I'd entered a gentleman's service.

"Aye, 'twill be a hot day. Here." Picking up his purse from where it lay on top of a heap of his clothing, he tossed me two pence. "Go downstairs and buy a loaf from Mistress Stavesly for breakfast. And some ale from the tavern on the corner. Enough for thyself as well."

I must harden myself, I thought, as I seized two tankards off the shelf and made my escape. I must somehow learn to act as if the sight of a half-naked man was nothing new to me. Or Master Marlowe would surely start to wonder why his new servant boy blushed so easily.

To my relief, when I returned with the loaf of bread still warm in my hands, Master Marlowe was dressed, not in the magnificent velvet he had worn yesterday, but in a plain workaday doublet of dark green broadcloth, his wet hair pulled neatly back to the nape of his neck.

I need not have been so scrupulous about not disturbing Master Marlowe's papers, for he simply swept them aside with one arm to clear a space on the table for the food. There was only the one stool, and I did not dare to claim a space, uninvited, at the table with my master. I took my bread and tankard of ale and sat on a corner of my pallet.

Master Marlowe was silent while he ate, the quick chatter of yesterday gone. *Changeable as March wind,* Mistress Stavesly had called him. I sat without speaking, so as not to disturb his mood, chewing the creamy yellow manchet bread with appreciation. It was fine and soft enough that it needed no butter to sweeten it.

"Well, then," Master Marlowe said when his meal was over, and he got up from the table. "Let me see thee prove thy boast."

I swallowed my last mouthful of bread hastily. My boast? I'd hardly said a word all morning. But when he nodded at the stool he had been sitting on, I understood what he meant.

Master Marlowe did not spare money on his work, I thought as I seated myself. The quills scattered about looked the best, made from the third or fourth wing feathers of a goose, and the paper he scribbled on so carelessly had probably cost two or three shillings for half a ream. I did not see the page with the strange symbols I had noticed earlier.

"Write this out for me," Master Marlowe said, pushing a sheet of paper over the table. I picked up a quill and frowned to find the point crushed and dull. A clerk must respect his pens, my father always said, as a carpenter respects his tools. A blunt knife is more likely to slip and cut you than a sharp one, and a blunt pen is more likely to skip and catch on the paper, scattering ink far and wide.

Luckily there was a small ivory-handled knife among the clutter on the tabletop. I was conscious of Master Marlowe watching critically as I cut the pen to a fresh, sharp point, but I did not let him hurry me. He propped a hip against the table and folded his arms while I licked my fingers, rubbed the pen's tip to soften it, and uncorked the tiny lead bottle.

The smell of the ink, sharp and bitter and black, made tears sting behind my eyes for just a moment. I could almost hear my father's voice, as if he stood behind me: "Good, i'faith, very good, Rosalind . . ." I blinked and looked over at the scribbled sheet of manuscript Master Marlowe had given me.

The first line was a speech for a character named Dumaine. I felt a chill creep into my heart as I saw what Master Marlowe expected me to write, and looked up from the page to find his steady eye on me.

"What is the play to be called, sir?" I asked, amazed to hear the smooth tone of my own voice.

"*The Massacre at Paris,*" Master Marlowe answered.

The Massacre. The time of horror, some twenty years ago, when French Catholics had murdered their Protestant neighbors in the streets.

I put my eyes back on the fresh, clean sheet of paper before me and steadied the pen in my hand. Did he know? Was he watching to see if my cheek would grow pale or my hand would tremble? I bit down on the inside of my lip and put the tip of the pen to the page. The ink flowed easily, the letters black and neat. I moved my hand slowly and smoothly, listening to the faint rasp of the quill against the paper, and looked back at the words I had written.

> DUMAINE: *I swear by this to be unmerciful.*
> ANJOU: *I am disguised, and none knows who I am,*
> *And therefore mean to murder all I meet.*

So this was what he thought of us—that we, the faithful, were murderers and traitors, thirsting for the blood of innocent Protestants. But I kept my face expressionless, my hand steady. If this were a trap, I would betray nothing. If it were no trap—if Master Marlowe truly had no idea what faith I cherished—then I must not give him the slightest hint.

"Let me see," said Master Marlowe, holding out a hand and snapping his fingers for the paper.

I blew gently on the wet ink, still glistening, and picked the page up by the edges to hand it to him. He took it delicately and raised an eyebrow while he studied it.

"So thou toldst truth. Where didst learn to write such a fair hand?"

"My father taught me, sir." My voice, respectful and mild, sounded like someone else's in my ears. What would my father have said, had he known that the pen he'd taught me to hold would write such words of my fellow Catholics?

"Well enough. I think I'll keep thee, Richard." Master Marlowe waved me off the stool and sat down himself. "When I'm done today, thou'lt write out the scenes I've finished. It will save me hiring a clerk for it." He shuffled the papers on the table, found what he was looking for, and began to scrawl on a fresh sheet, pressing down so hard that my nicely cut pen was reduced to a shapeless blob in an instant. I watched him for a moment, but he seemed to have forgotten that I was in the room.

After a while I took up Mistress Stavesly's broom again.

I swept the bedroom and straightened the bed and emptied the bowl of water out the window. Then, reluctantly, I picked up the chamber pot. A few weeks ago, I would never have touched such an object. But now . . .

Now, I told myself firmly, I had no choice. But still, I could not keep my nose from wrinkling as the stinking contents of the pot followed the wash water out into the street. I wiped my hands on my doublet and turned thankfully to more pleasant tasks, picking up Master Marlowe's clothes from the floor. The buttons on his velvet doublet clinked softly together as I brushed and folded it and laid it, along with his breeches and hose and linen shirt and collar, away in the chest. I wondered if I could find a rag to dust with.

"Richard!"

I jumped. "Yes, master?" I came into the doorway between the two rooms to find Master Marlowe scowling at me.

"Thou'lt fidget me beyond endurance. Go away."

"Yes, master." I hesitated. "When should I return?"

"An hour. Two. What thou wilt." He turned his attention back to the paper on the table, but I was bold enough to speak again.

"May I have your leave to visit my father, sir?"

"Thou hast my leave to visit the devil, so thou dost it elsewhere than here," he said impatiently. "Stay!" I had started for the door, but he got up suddenly and stalked into the bedchamber. When he came back, he tossed something to me, something small and round that flashed in the light as it flew through the air. I caught it between my hands. It was a shilling.

"An advance on thy wages," Master Marlowe said,

sitting back down. "Thou'lt need it to give to the jailer. Take it and begone."

I snatched up Mistress Stavesly's broom and all but ran out the door before his abrupt generosity could reverse itself.

Mistress Stavesly lifted her eyebrows when I returned the broom and asked her the way to Newgate Prison. But she told me how to find it, and kept a customer waiting to be sure that I understood her directions. Eagerly I set off into the London streets.

Already everything seemed less strange, the crowds less threatening. My new clothing, which had made me feel so bare and vulnerable yesterday, in truth rendered me nearly invisible. I was just another shabby servant boy in a city full of them. No one paid me the slightest heed.

I made my way down Bishopsgate Street, as Mistress Stavesly had told me. But where Threadneedle Street branched off to the southwest, I hesitated.

By all rights I should continue south, cross the bridge, and go to the playhouse to find Robin. I was still angry with him, and yet—it was his father, too.

But Master Henslowe had said there would be rehearsal in the morning, and I had only an hour or two to spare. If I made my way across the river now, and then

Robin could not go to Newgate with me, I would have spent nearly half the time I had, and to no purpose.

And besides, I needed to speak to my father about Robin, about how to coax or reason or order him out of the playhouse. I could hardly do that with my brother present.

I set off, determined, down Threadneedle Street. After all, if Robin was busy learning his new trade, that was his own choice and no fault of mine. I broke into a run, as if I could outpace the shreds of guilt that still clung to my heels.

By the time I reached the broad avenue of Cheapside, I was out of breath and had to slow to a walk again. I passed shops selling hats, stockings, lace, birdcages, buttons, needles, earrings. None of it held any interest for me. I could see the back of St. Paul's Cathedral to my left, rising over walls and rooftops, but I hardly spared it a glance.

What will our father say when he sees thee? What could I tell him, how could I explain my breeches and doublet? I could not reveal what had nearly happened to me two days ago. It would break his heart to know of the danger I had been in, the disgrace he could no longer protect me from.

What-will-I-tell-him, what-will-I-tell-him jogged in my mind to the rhythm of my feet upon the paving stones as I turned up Newgate Street. No ideas came into my head, but I found I hardly cared. It did not matter. Nothing mattered except seeing my father at last.

There was the prison. My quick steps slowed a little. The street led straight up to the prison's gateway, and I felt as if I stood in a river with my legs braced against a current that wanted to sweep me away through that gate and into the darkness beyond.

Mere fancy. It was just a heavy stone building, built over the roadway as if there had not been enough space for it elsewhere. It was foolish to let dread churn in my stomach. I'd known well enough my father was in prison. I could not let the sight of that prison, looming dark over the street, stop me in my tracks.

There was a door set in one wall of the dark tunnel underneath the building. As I approached it, a filthy hand, no more than skin drawn tight over bones and knuckles, shot out of a barred window to seize hold of my elbow.

"For pity's sake, some bread," a voice whined. "Have mercy, young sir, 'twill be to the credit of your soul. . . ."

I fought back the urge to shriek and wrench my arm away. My father might be reduced to this one day. No, I would never let that happen. But still, I answered civilly.

"I am sorry, friend. I have nothing to give."

The hand dragged me closer to the bars, and in the

dimness inside I could see a wolfish face, as thin as the hand, half hidden in greasy hair and a long, straggling beard. "Have pity," the prisoner begged, as if he had not heard a word I'd said.

"I am sorry, I—"

"Pity! Pity!"

"I have nothing!" I pulled my arm away; although the man clung desperately, he had no strength to hold me. Other hands were thrust out of the window, other voices pleaded. Guilt clutched at my throat. I had still a few coins in my purse, and a master who, strange though he might be, would probably feed me tonight. Should I give all I had to these starving wretches? But I could not. I needed—my father needed—what little money I had. Shutting my ears to the calls for bread and meat and mercy, I hurried past the window to the heavy oak door, bound with iron.

"Pardon, master," I said to an old man who sat slumped on a stool by the door. One of his legs, thrust out into the street before him, ended above the knee, with a wooden peg strapped on. He squinted up at me under thick white eyebrows and said nothing.

"I wish to visit a—" My voice, already shaken, choked a little on the word. But this was no time for weakness. "A prisoner," I finished, as steadily as I could. "May I go in?"

The one-legged man held out a hand to me, palm uppermost. His skin was gray, creased with deep lines of black dirt. I blinked in surprise.

"Halfpence for the doorkeeper," he wheezed at me impatiently.

Oh. I fumbled with my purse and drew out a half-penny, which I dropped into the waiting hand, and Master Marlowe's shilling, which I clutched tightly. The old man, with a groan, heaved himself to his feet and limped over to the door. He took out a key on a chain around his neck and worked it in the lock for at least a minute while my heart thumped and my feet twitched. *Let me in, let me in,* my mind whispered, in time to the beat of blood in my veins.

The lock clicked open at last. I pushed past the door-keeper and nearly tumbled down a flight of stone stairs that led to a long, dark hallway with another door at the end.

"Wait!" I called back up the stairs. "Where should I go?"

"To thy left!" the old man answered impatiently, and heaved the heavy door shut with a solid clang that shook me to my bones.

The air was damp and hot and thick, and it smelled like a privy and something worse. A slaughterhouse.

Blood and corruption. I put a hand over my mouth and looked to my left. Now I saw an open door, halfway down the hall. When I entered, I found a tiny closet of a room with a single small window. Even the sunlight that streamed through that square hole, bare of glass, seemed greasy and dull. A short, squat man, half bald, sat at a table with a book open before him. The pages were brown, scattered with spots of ink and candle grease. He looked up at me and grunted a question.

"Please, master, I wish to see Robert Archer." I shut my hand hard around Master Marlowe's shilling. The metal had warmed to the temperature of my skin; the sharp edge of the coin bit into my palm.

The jailer sucked his teeth and put out a hand. I gave him the shilling. He looked it over carefully, rubbed it, nibbled it, and seemed satisfied at last, dropping it into a small iron box on the table before turning to the book.

He flipped over a few pages and ran his thumb down the paper. "Archer, Archer. Robert. Here." He stopped and looked up at me. "A papist." I nodded. The man shrugged and put his thumb in his mouth to chew on the nail.

"Dead," he said indifferently, and spat out a shred of thumbnail. "Of the flux. A week or so ago. A fair lot of them had it, and a right mess it was. The cells still stink of it. Here, hold up, boy."

I had to put both hands out and grasp the edge of the table to keep myself from falling.

"One less papist in the world's nothing to grieve for," the jailer said. "Friend of thine, was he?" And his eyes ranged over my face, coldly suspicious.

I did not answer him. My jaw was locked, my tongue cold and heavy in my mouth. Somehow I made my way outside into the sunlight. But the smell of the prison stayed with me, and its thick, damp air clung to my skin.

Slowly, a little unsteadily, I began to walk back the way that I had come.

What a flat, cold, ugly word. "Dead." Such a short word to destroy everything that was left of my life.

It could not be true. We could not have come so far, struggled so hard, lost so much, for *nothing*. I felt hollow inside, as if my skin were only a fragile shell over black emptiness. The next person to knock against me in the crowded streets would shatter me into pieces. There would be nothing left.

We had fled home, Robin and I, and walked so many miles south to London. We had lost our money, I had thrown away my name and my modesty, Robin was courting blasphemy at a playhouse, all so we could be near our father. And none of it was worth the effort it had cost.

"God keep thee safe, Rosalind," he'd whispered, holding

me as if he would keep everything evil away by the strength of his arms. But he could not protect me anymore. I was alone, and the street beneath me was not a river anymore; it was a whirlpool, black and deep, sure to drag me down.

He could not keep me safe. He could not keep himself so. What had been the point, then, to all those years of faithfulness? Of the priests that my father had hidden in that tiny room? Of the prayers and the secret candles to the saints, if none of it helped him? Where had they been, his saints, when he had died alone and unshriven, not even knowing if his children were safe?

No, no, I dared not think so. I realized with a jolt how close I had come to the edge of blasphemy. With my father's soul perhaps now in purgatory, how dared I even think reproach to the saints? "Forgive me, forgive me," I murmured under my breath. "Forgive me, have mercy."

I was jostled and pushed and fell more than once. I often lost my way, but I did not ask for help. I simply kept walking. At last, more by accident than anything else, I struck the broad street that led up to Bishopsgate, and made my way north to Master Marlowe's lodgings.

I stood for some time in the street, staring at the building, until it occurred to me that I ought to climb the stairs. There had not seemed so many of them before. When I reached the top at last, Master Marlowe came out of his bedroom, frowning.

"I gave thee leave to visit Newgate, not the antipodes, Richard. Hast been wandering about London at thine ease?" He was wearing the black velvet doublet again, I noticed without interest, and a pearl earring in one ear.

"Richard?"

I rubbed my hands up and down my arms. It was very strange how cold it was, for the end of summer, just before the harvest. I should not have been shivering.

Master Marlowe came closer. Gently he put two fingers under my chin, tipping my head back so that he could see my face.

"Art ill? Richard, what is't?"

"My father's dead," I told him. The words reminded me of bits of ice in the river when it had just started to freeze, bobbing and swirling by themselves in the cold gray water.

With his hand on my shoulder, Master Marlowe steered me over to my pallet in the corner. He pushed me down. My knees had no strength to resist. He took a blanket and wrapped it around my shoulders, guiding my hand so that it held two corners together at my throat. Then he was gone, clattering down the stairs.

After some time he was back again, pushing a wooden tankard into my hands. The cup was hot. He moved it up toward my face. I smelled sweet wine, cinnamon, honey. It burned my throat when I swallowed.

Still without speaking, Master Marlowe sat back on his heels and studied me for a moment. He rose swiftly and left again, only to reappear almost at once, with Moll in tow.

"Sit thee down," Master Marlowe said to her, giving her a push in the direction of my pallet. "Do not speak to him, just wait for me." And he left the room once more.

Obedient as a dog, Moll didn't try to talk to me, or ask how I did, or even inquire what was happening. She seemed content just to sit, doing nothing, hardly moving, as if breathing were enough of an occupation for her.

When Master Marlowe came back for the third time, he brought Robin with him. My brother's face was smudged with dirt and tears.

"Come, Moll, good lass," Master Marlowe said quietly. "Let's leave them now." Moll patted me gently on the arm, like she might a sick puppy, and followed Master Marlowe out of the room.

"Rosalind?" Robin knelt down by the pallet. "He—he told me. How couldst thou go without me? Do not look so. Art angry with me? I am sorry for what I said. I did not mean it." The pitch of his voice grew higher, and new tears spilled down his cheeks. "Rosalind, speak a word to me. Rosalind, please?"

Then I began to cry at last.

chapter six
august 1592

When I woke the next morning, I lay still, looking at the slanted ceiling above me. I wished I had not woken. How pleasant it would be to lie in this bed until the Last Judgment came.

But I could not. I had a duty, and one that must be finished before Master Marlowe was stirring. I threw back the blanket, dressed quickly, and knelt beside my pallet.

I'd failed my father once. I had not reached London in time to help him. The money I'd lost my first day in this city would have moved him to a better cell, would have paid for food and blankets, would have brought a doctor to him. It might have saved him.

It was too late for that now. But I could at least do what I might for his soul. I was no priest; I could not say Mass, but I whispered, as quickly as possible, the few words that I knew, asking for remembrance, for mercy. "*Memento etiam, Domine . . ."* Remember my father, please. Keep him safe, as he could not keep me. The Latin words slurred together in my hurry, but it did not matter. God would understand.

I had barely murmured "Amen" and crossed myself when a voice spoke behind me. "Awake early, art thou?"

I flinched as if Master Marlowe's voice had been a thunderclap. But my back was to him. He could not have seen me make the sign of the cross. And surely he could not have overheard my whispered prayer. Rubbing his hands over his face and squinting in the light, he did not appear to have noticed anything amiss. Mercifully he was dressed more thoroughly than yesterday, with a shirt hanging loose over his hose.

"Fetch water," he said shortly, barely looking at me. There was nothing of yesterday's gentleness in his tone. The day before he had gotten leave for Robin to stay away from the playhouse, and had not asked any work of me, letting us mourn together. But clearly his kindness had its limits.

I brought water for Master Marlowe to wash, and food to break his fast, and borrowed Mistress Stavesly's broom again, watching my hands go through these servant's tasks as if they belonged to someone else. How strange it was. My father was dead, and yet I must fetch and carry and clean. I must breathe and my heart must beat, even though I would never see my father again until I died myself.

Then all might yet be well. Then he might take me in his arms, declaring that he'd missed me terribly, that he'd wept for grief every night.

But in the meantime, there was still this day to live, and tomorrow, and only God knew how many more. I became aware that there were tears on my cheeks and that Master Marlowe, who sat at his table writing, had lifted his head from his work and was steadily watching me.

"I envy thee," he said quietly, when I stopped sweeping and looked up. "My father lives in Canterbury. I've hardly seen him since I left the university and came to London to write plays. If he were gone, I would not weep for him. Nor he, I am sure, for me."

Then he looked back down at his work, and began to write busily once more, as if he had never spoken.

I lived my first days in London in a haze of grief, as if I had suddenly been struck half blind, half deaf, and as slow-witted as Moll. I walked into doorjambs and tripped over cobblestones and often did not hear when someone spoke to me.

Robin, when I saw him as I accompanied Master

Marlowe to the playhouse, let tears fall easily as he spoke about our father. "Dost remember the wooden horse he carved for me, with the short front leg?" he would say. "Dost remember when the pigs got into the garden, and he chased them out again, and fell in the mud, how he laughed? Dost remember?"

I would nod wearily. Yes, I remembered. But I had few tears to shed and no stories to add to his. I was only tired, so tired that it seemed I could never sleep enough. Only a night that lasted until the end of the world would be long enough for me.

I had tried so hard to take care of Robin, to take care of us both, to keep things as they should have been. But I had failed, that was all. Nothing more was to be done. Now I must learn to live the rest of my life in sorrow, as simply and naturally as a fish lived in the sea.

Early one afternoon I came back from an errand to find Master Marlowe sitting at his table as usual, scribbling away. "Ah, Richard," he said, looking up. "Good, I have finished the last sheet of paper. And didst get the new pens also?"

I took half a ream of fresh paper out of the basket I carried over my shoulder and set it down on the table, staring stupidly at it. Had he said he wanted pens as well?

"Thou didst not buy them?"

"I am sorry, sir," I said dully.

"God's teeth—" Master Marlowe sighed. "Never mind it. Thou hast been in my service a week, Richard. Didst know that?"

Had it been so much as a week? I was vaguely surprised to hear it.

"I'm well enough pleased with thy work," he went on, rifling through the stack of paper on the table and not looking up at me. "I'll take thee on a year's contract, if thou'rt willing."

There was a reason, I thought, why I had not wished to stay in Master Marlowe's service. Oh yes. He was a play-maker, a blasphemer, with a careless tongue and a strange manner. I had planned to search for other work, for my brother and myself.

But the idea of going out into the street, asking strangers if they knew of servant's work elsewhere, made me want to weep with weariness. And what did it matter now? I had no family left to be shamed by my service to a playmaker.

"Aye, master," I said indifferently. But then a thought stirred in my mind. For the first time since I had learned of my father's death, I gave consideration to something besides myself. It occurred to me that I had not proven to be of much value. That any other master would surely have cast out such a lackwitted, ham-handed, idle, and forgetful servant as a bad bargain, and not offered me a year's worth of food and clothes and wages.

"I thank you for your kindness, sir," I said belatedly, my gratitude little better than an afterthought.

Master Marlowe took up a new sheet of paper, smoothed it with his hand, and began to write.

"I told thee before, 'tis not kindness," he said before he blew on the paper to dry the ink and folded it in half. "Take this to Henslowe at the Rose. And have the goodness, pray, to buy those pens on thy way back, or I shall be reduced to dipping a finger in the ink."

When I arrived at the Rose, I found one of the playhouse's hirelings struggling to peel off a large sheet of paper that had been pasted up by the door. It was a libel, printed in bold black letters for everyone who could to read:

PLAYS CAUSE PLAGUE

"'Twas pasted up overnight," said John, the porter, when he saw me looking. "Puritans, no doubt. For all the good it does them, when they know 'twill be down in the morning. Thou'rt Kit Marlowe's boy, art not?" He waved me inside.

Master Henslowe was sitting in the gallery to watch the

rehearsal. When I handed him Master Marlowe's message, he read it, sighed heavily, and told me to wait until he had a moment to write a response.

I sat myself down on the far side of the yard, away from the stage, and wrapped my arms around my knees, hugging my warmth to myself.

Where was Robin? I didn't see him. Perhaps I should go search for him. But it was pleasant just now to sit and let my mind rest. I laid my head down on my knees, feeling the heat of the sun across my back and shoulders.

A rich voice drifted into my awareness. It was deep and smooth, caressing the words it spoke as if it loved them. It did not seem loud, yet I heard every word distinctly, as if the speaker knelt beside me.

> *"Ah, good my lord, be patient; she is dead,*
> *And all this raging cannot make her live.*
> *If words might serve, our voice hath rent the air;*
> *If tears, our eyes have watered all the earth;*
> *If grief, our murdered hearts have strain'd*
>   *forth blood.*
> *Nothing prevails, for she is dead, my lord."*

That was right, it was true. How did he know?

My eyes stung as I lifted up my head to see the stage

through a strange haze. The paint and gilt swam in a mist of brightness, red and gold, blue and green. Some of the colors moved and gestured and became people as I blinked and a tear or two slipped down my cheeks. There were men in doublets of red brocade or tunics of yellow satin, bearing helmets and swords that caught the sun in bursts of light. The swirl of color centered around a plain, dark figure who knelt in dejection by a bed on which a woman lay, her white gown spilling like milk to the floor.

'Tis beautiful, I thought. *God's truth, 'tis beautiful.*

Then I blinked again and saw more clearly that it was Master Alleyn kneeling, in a plain, dark doublet, the only one on stage not in costume. Master Cowley stood beside him, a hand on his shoulder, and I thought it was he who'd just spoken, as if he'd plucked the grief out of my heart and shaped it into words. The boy Harry, in the gorgeous white gown, his eyes closed, lay gracefully across the bed on cushions of black and gold.

There was a long silence. Then Master Alleyn spoke.

"I beg your pardon, masters. What is next?"

Harry opened one eye and snorted. Master Alleyn threatened him with a gloved hand, and he promptly shut both eyes and lay still.

"'For she is dead,'" prompted a thin, anxious-looking man who sat cross-legged on a corner of the stage, hunched over the manuscript in his lap.

"Ah, yes," said Master Alleyn. "'For she is dead? Thy words do pierce my soul. . . .'"

"Richard? Richard Archer?"

I looked up to see a tall, gangly young apprentice standing before me. He had light brown hair that he pushed out of his eyes with one hand, a shy smile, and a folded piece of paper in one hand.

"I'm Sander Ramsey," he said, holding the paper out to me. "Master Henslowe sent me to find you. He says to take this answer to Master Marlowe."

"I thank you," I murmured, and got to my feet, taking the message. To my surprise, I saw that Sander was holding something else out to me, something that sat red and glossy bright in the palm of his other hand. An apple.

"I'm lodged with Master Cowley," he said awkwardly, as if this explained why he should offer a gift to a stranger. "With Robin. Your brother. He told us about your father. I'm sorry for it, truly."

An apple, as if that could make up for the raw loss of a father. But Sander looked anxious, and a little embarrassed, and I knew he was only trying to be kind.

Kindness was not a quality I'd looked to find in a playhouse.

"And Robin said he'd meet you outside the playhouse,"

Sander went on. "He said he'd wait for you there."

"I thank you," I said again, confused, as I took the gift from his hand. Why should Robin wait for me in the street, as if he had a secret? "For the apple and the message."

Sander grinned. "I must go, there's a lesson starting," he said. "Tell Robin not to be late." And he ran toward the stage as I made my way out the playhouse door. As Sander had said, Robin was waiting for me, looking uneasy.

"Robin? Art well?"

"Aye, well," he said, and shrugged. "Ill. Both. And thou?"

I smiled, for the first time, it seemed, in days. I almost felt the skin of my face cracking, like thin ice. "The same."

Robin shifted his feet a little, scuffing at the dusty cobblestones.

"Sander says there's a lesson starting," I said. "Thou'lt be late."

"Aye, I know."

"Robin? What is't?"

"I must tell thee."

"What, in heaven's name?"

"Master Henslowe said my week of trial's over." Robin looked up at me at last. "He says I'm shaping well. I can stay."

So that was why he seemed so doubtful, almost afraid.

"'Tis not like being a fortune-teller or a tumbler at the fairs." Robin burst into speech before I could say anything at all. "Master Henslowe owns the Rose himself. He's very nearly rich! And Master Marlowe studied at Oxford! They are gentlemen, truly. And—"

I held up a hand. "Robin, listen a moment."

He paid no heed. "'Tis a trade like any other. There's no disgrace in honest work. And I can do it well."

"*Honest?*" I repeated. Truly I had not meant to quarrel with him, but I could not keep a sarcastic twist from my voice. "Honest to lie for a living?"

It was a mistake. Robin's jaw tightened.

"'Tis my own choice to make," he said mulishly.

"But, Robin, think a moment." Argument, I knew, would be wasted, but honeyed words might still sway him. "Thou'rt a merchant's son—"

"No longer."

The truth of that stopped my words in my throat.

The stubborn expression had melted off Robin's face. He only seemed sorrowful, and older than his years. I blinked in surprise to see my younger brother look so much like a man. So much like our father.

"I would not quarrel with thee," he said simply. "But I want to stay. I will stay."

And what was I to answer? The choice was plain before me. I could accept Robin's decision or I could quarrel with him. But either way he would not leave the playhouse behind.

Robin was all the family I had left. I could not bear to be at enmity with him, not now. Not after everything else I had lost.

I sighed. "Stay, then."

Robin looked startled. "Thou dost not mind it?"

I did mind it. But I could see no help for it. So I gave voice to another lie and took yet another sin upon my head.

"I do not mind it." But something else still seemed to trouble my brother. "What is't?" I asked.

"Master Cowley—" He shifted his feet uneasily, and suddenly looked his years again, and guilt-stricken. "Master Cowley says we must all to church on Sundays. 'Tis well? Should I go?"

"I think thou must," I said, resigned. "There is no other way." Robin still looked worried. "God sees thy heart, Robin. Keep thou the true faith there. Dost pray for Father's soul?"

"Every night, I swear."

"And say thy beads?"

He nodded.

"Robin Archer!" Sander appeared at the playhouse door. "Master Cowley says thou'lt have no supper if thou dost not come back!"

"Go on," I told him. And he surprised me mightily by throwing his arms tightly around me. "God keep thee safe," he whispered, before running back inside the play-house after Sander.

I set off, turning my steps toward the bridge and back to the rooms I supposed I must begin to call home, remembering this time to stop at a stationer's and buy new pens for Master Marlowe. I thought that I should feel overcome with shame, now that it was irrevocable I must have a player for a brother. But strangely, I did not. Perhaps grief swamps all other feelings, leaving no room for guilt or bitterness.

Sander's apple was still in my hand. Its skin was satin smooth as I rubbed it with my fingers, a fresh red tinged with green. I bit into it, tasting the rush of juice in my mouth, sharp and sweet at once. I did not know why it should make my eyes sting with tears for the second time that morning, or why it should make me feel somehow comforted.

chapter seven
september 1592

Before I had been in London a month, the heat of
summer started to die and a chill crept into the evenings.
But by midday the air was still warm as summer, and on
one such day Master Marlowe took a fancy to have a wash.

He sent me to the conduit for water, and kindled a coal
fire himself to heat it. I struggled up the stairs with the
heavy bucket, biting my lip and trying to think of some
excuse I might use to leave the room before the dreadful
moment when he would strip off his clothes.

Mornings were bad enough, but Master Marlowe gen-
erally dressed himself in his bedchamber, and I could find
some task that would keep my eyes elsewhere until he had
finished. This, however . . .

It was ridiculous to clean the whole body at once, I
thought. It would no doubt make him ill. Back home we'd
bathed in the river now and again in the summer, and

thought of nothing else. Of course, no one in London would choose to swim in the filth of the Thames. Still, it could not be wise of my master to expose himself so recklessly to all sorts of fevers and sickness. Next the foolish man would be wanting to wash his hair.

Panting, I reached the lodgings, emptied my bucket into the pot over the fire, and wondered if I could feign an illness that would confine me to the privy for the next hour or so. Then I heard footsteps on the stairs.

"Kit! News!" The door swung hard enough on its hinges to bang into the wall, and the man who stood in the doorway was breathing quickly from his climb. "Listen, Kit—"

He stopped abruptly. I recognized him, a dark, handsome man in an emerald green doublet, his face frowning between a crisp white ruff and a hat with a tall crown. Master Marlowe's friend Tom Watson. I had last seen him at the playhouse, leaning on the railing of the gallery, jesting about the devil.

"And if there is news, need you shout it for all the street to hear?" Master Marlowe demanded, coming out of his bedchamber in his shirt and breeches, untying the ruff around his neck. "Henslowe will have you on stage at the Rose; your voice is loud enough for it. Richard." His attention shifted suddenly to me, and he twitched the ruff loose and tossed it in my direction. "Take that and have it starched. My cuffs also. Go, get them from the chest."

I blinked, looking at the bathwater heating over the fire, at the large porcelain bowl with the soap and the linen towels laid out next to it. "But—do you not wish me to fetch more water?" He would need cold, to mix with the hot, or he'd scald his skin as well as catch his death.

"No, I wish thee to go to the laundry," Master Marlowe snapped. "And when thou'rt done, get me a book as well. Hotman's history of France. The bookseller will know it. And bring it to me at the Rose. Go on, hurry, do I pay thee to drag thy feet?"

My knees felt watery with relief, and I certainly was not inclined to argue any further. Tom Watson had moved over to the table and stood without speaking, rifling through the papers there, as I collected Master Marlowe's linen in a basket and sixpence for the book. The heel from a loaf of bread was sitting on the windowsill, left over from the morning meal. I slipped it into the basket as well. Master Marlowe did not notice.

"Does he know nothing?" I heard Master Watson say as I shut the door behind me, and then an angry sound, not quite a word, as if Master Marlowe wished to silence him.

Mistress Stavesly had been right to call Master Marlowe changeable, I thought, as I made my way down the stairs. To tell me to prepare a bath, and then send me from the room so suddenly, as if—

Well, and what if Master Marlowe wished to speak to his friend in private? Surely that was not so unusual. Any master might desire to keep some matters from a servant's ears.

It was no concern of mine. But still I could not quite forget it, and tucked it away in my mind along with other of Master Marlowe's peculiarities. There was his luxurious clothing, for one, and his poor, bare lodgings. There were the many nights he stumbled up the stairs after the bells had rung for nine o'clock, smelling of ale and sack and burnt wine. Or the way he slept late on Sunday mornings and never seemed to see the inside of a church. In a way this last was a comfort to me, since it meant I might avoid church as well, and not risk my soul at the Protestant service. I was only a servant, and if my master did not make me attend church, no one else was likely to do it. But Master Marlowe was well known; how was it that he could flout the law with indifference?

Well, it was not my affair. I was his servant, not his keeper or his confessor, and it would be impudence in me to wonder about the state of his soul. My only concern was to get his linen cleaned and starched, and for that I made my way to the Dutch neighborhood just south of Bishopsgate.

Mistress Pieters, the laundress, was talking closely with a man as I arrived, as fair-haired and blue eyed as she was. Her shop was full of the harsh, soapy scent of starch and a bitter, scorched smell from the metal rods heating in the fire, ready to iron ruffs smooth once they had been cleaned.

"'Tis talk, nothing more," Mistress Pieters said briskly, but she did not sound certain about it. Her milk-pale skin was flushed red with the heat of her work.

"More than talk," the man said, shaking his head. "Jan van der Berg's son was found beaten in an alleyway, half dead."

"Thieves," Mistress Pieters said firmly. "Plenty of cut-purses abroad in London without— Good day, Richard. Thy master must have his cuffs cleaned yet again?"

The man frowned at me and said something in a language I did not understand. Mistress Pieters answered him shortly in the same tongue. Dutch, it must be.

"And his ruff, too," I said, taking the articles out of my basket and handing them over. The thin lawn fabric looked clean enough to me, but I was not the one who had to wear it.

"Wait and see, then," the man said to Mistress Pieters, brushing past me on his way out of the shop.

Mistress Pieters paid him no heed. "Thank heaven for men's vanity, or I should beg on the streets," she said cheerfully, holding the delicate white linen to the light with her red, roughened hands.

"Wait and see about what?" I asked her, looking back the way the Dutch man had gone.

"'Tis nothing," Mistress Pieters said briskly, folding Master Marlowe's linen neatly away into a basket. "Idle talk on the streets. Some folk do not love newcomers, especially those from Holland."

I frowned, baffled. "But you are a Protestant," I said, without thinking.

"Aye, and what does that matter?"

"I thought . . ." I wavered, confused. Considering how the English treated Catholics, I would have thought they'd welcome Dutch Protestants fleeing the war Catholic Spain was this moment waging in the Low Countries. "I thought they would not mind it," I finished weakly. "Other Protestants, I mean."

"There are always some who do not like outsiders," Mistress Pieters answered. "But if we work hard and pay our taxes to the city, they will not trouble us." She smiled cheerfully at me. "And pray, what would the English do, if the Dutch went back to Holland and took the secret of starching with us? Their ruffs would be drooping down to their armpits. Come back tomorrow, and I will have these ready for thee."

I made my way down Broad Street, past the Dutch church where Mistress Pieters and the other immigrants prayed on Sundays, and turned on Bucklesberrie, with the grocers and pepperers and the luscious smell of spices in the air. All the way I found myself twisting my thoughts into a tangle over what Mistress Pieters had told me. English Protestants, it seemed, did not care for foreign Protestants any more than they cared for native-born Catholics. I could not claim to understand it. What harm did Mistress Pieters do, starching cuffs and collars and ruffs in her little shop? What harm had my father done, praying to the saints? Why were they all so frightened, as if a country wool merchant and a Dutch laundress could threaten the state of England?

I gave it up as too hard a question when I came in sight of St. Paul's. As I made my way to the churchyard and the bookseller's stalls, I saw that the old veteran was there again, begging by the gate. He had been wounded, no doubt, in the very wars that drove Mistress Pieters from her home. An ugly scar marred half his face, a rag around his head covered the ruin of what had once been an eye, and his right hand was crippled and useless.

His son was with him today, a boy half Robin's age,

huddled by his father's side. I reached into the basket for the crust of bread I'd put there this morning. I always tried to bring a bite of food with me if I knew I'd have an errand near the churchyard.

"Good day to you," I said, and bent down to offer the bread to the little boy. His eyes widened eagerly, but he painstakingly divided it in half and handed one piece to his father before he took a bite.

The old veteran never spoke; perhaps he could not. But he nudged the boy, who mumbled, "Thank you, master," through his mouthful.

"Thou'rt welcome," I said. "I am sorry 'tis not more." And leaving them absorbed in this meager meal, I made my way to the stationer's in the churchyard.

At the stall with the pistol on the sign, the bookseller was helping an elegant young man find *The Art of the Fence,* to improve his swordplay. "A moment," he said, with a nod to me. "That was kind. Thou'rt the first this morning to give something."

"'Twill only encourage the man in beggary," the gentleman said, giving me a disdainful look.

"'Twas but a piece of bread," I answered. My eyes fell on the man's black kidskin gloves, pinked around the cuffs to show the lining of bright blue silk through tiny heart-shaped holes. The cost of one of those gloves would have fed the old veteran and his son for a year.

"No bread's due to the idle," he insisted.

Idle! I felt my temper rising. "He has only one eye and one hand," I objected. "What work is he fit for?"

"Here's your book, master," the bookseller intervened, and gave me a frown as the gentleman departed. "Art here to buy, lad, or simply to argue with my customers?"

I bought the book Master Marlowe had wanted. The beggar family was gone by the time I left the churchyard again and turned my steps toward the Rose.

I greeted John, who nodded me in, and saw Robin, in the midst of a tumbling lesson on the stage. I waved to him. He could not wave back, being in the middle of a handstand, but he smiled.

"Looking for Master Marlowe?" asked Sander, who stood in the yard before the stage. "He's in the galleries, I think, with Master Henslowe." He was juggling three apples as he spoke, and never took his eyes off them. "Watch this, now, tell me if 'tis good." One apple flew up higher than the others, well above his head. On the way down he snatched it, took a bite, and sent it spinning about with the rest.

I clapped for him. "Very good, i'faith." Sander took a second bite out of the apple and dropped all three to bounce and roll at his feet. He sighed, the boys onstage laughed, and I climbed the stairs to find Master Marlowe.

He was sitting in one of the second galleries, talking with Henslowe and another man. "And your new play, William? *Henry VI?*" Master Marlowe was asking the stranger as I came up to them. "How comes it?"

"Well, thank you, Kit." The man glanced at me. He had a calm manner and mild brown eyes. "Someone to see you, I think."

Master Marlowe turned around to regard me. "Well, Richard? Didst get the book?"

"Yes, sir." As I handed it to him, I could not help glancing at him, curious. Had he taken his bath? Maybe he'd thought better of it, and only washed his face.

"Excellent." He flipped through the book and then waved a dismissive hand at me. "I do not need thee at the moment. Thou'rt welcome to visit thy brother, if Master Henslowe will permit it."

"'Tis dinnertime at any rate," Master Henslowe said. "Aye, stay and welcome, lad. It does the boy good to see thee. Master Cowley says he is shaping well."

"Of course, since I found him for you." Master Marlowe tossed me a silver penny from his purse. "Buy thyself some food with the crackropes, Richard, and then make thy way home before the performance begins."

At the foot of the stairs, I hesitated, the penny clutched

in my hand. Master Marlowe had told me to eat with the apprentices. But I'd always tried to stay away from the other boys at the Rose and visit with Robin in private. They might notice something odd about me. They might suspect. Would it be better to make my own way home and try to see my brother later?

"Richard!" Robin called from behind me, ruining my cautious plans. The tumbling lesson had ended, and the boys were trooping together toward the playhouse door. "Stay and eat with us, canst thou?"

No graceful way to avoid it now. "Aye," I said, following him outside. I was probably too anxious in any case. After all, I had been Richard for nearly a month now, and no one—not Master Marlowe, not Mistress Stavesly— seemed to suspect. Why should the boys be any wiser? I would simply stay quiet and draw no notice. Easily done. Players, even apprentice ones, were too fond of attention themselves to spare much of it for others.

One of the older boys, Nat, bought meat pies from an ordinary near the playhouse. I bought one for myself with Master Marlowe's penny, and we settled down on the grass near the Rose to eat our meal.

"Where's Harry?" Sander asked, before he stuffed his mouth with half his meat pie at once.

"Rehearsing with Master Alleyn," Nat answered.

"Too grand to eat with the crackropes," one of the other boys said at the same time. "Have you ever seen his like for pride, since he got this part?"

"You live with Master Marlowe, then?" one of the younger boys—Sam, I thought his name was—asked, changing the conversation as he turned to me. All my plans to stay quiet and unnoticed fell into ruin with this simple question. "What is he like, truly?"

Now all the boys were looking at me as I bit down through the tough pastry of my pie into the salty, savory filling, and wiped gravy from my mouth with the back of my hand. I tried to find a quick answer, something to satisfy them and let the talk turn elsewhere. "He's—" *Changeable as March wind.* "Full of strange moods. But he's been a good master to me."

This did not seem to be what Sam wanted to know. "But is it true that he's"—his voice dropped to a dramatic whisper—"an atheist?"

I swallowed too large a mouthful and nearly choked. "*No!* No, I am sure—" I faltered a moment. Certainly Master Marlowe avoided church. But that might mean no more than carelessness—or something else. My father himself had gone to church as rarely as he dared, and left before Communion, for the safety of his soul. I forgot to answer Sam as a new thought struck me.

Could it be that Master Marlowe had some reason other than late nights and a sore head for avoiding church on Sundays? Could he, by any chance, be a secret Catholic himself?

"I heard he conjures the devil at night," Sam persisted.

"He does no such thing!" I objected, and only then remembered the piece of paper, covered with strange symbols, that I had seen on Master Marlowe's table. But I could not afford to have them all thinking I served a magician or a witch.

"Harry swears he counted an extra man on stage once in *Faustus*," one of the other boys put in.

"Master Alleyn says 'Nonsense,'" Nat countered.

"Well, 'tis true enough that someone was killed during *Tamburlaine*," Sam went on, hungry for scandal of some kind. "Sander, were you there?"

"I was not," Sander answered regretfully, "but I heard of it. 'Tis the scene, you know, where they kill the governor, and somehow the pistol was loaded." He made a gun of his thumb and forefinger and pointed it dramatically at Robin's head. "The shot went wide into the audience, and two were killed."

"But how came it the gun was loaded?" I could not keep from asking.

Sander shrugged. "No one knows, nor could ever

find out. They said the play was cursed. We sold every seat in the house for months."

And that seemed to satisfy them all. What did two deaths matter, if the galleries were full?

"But Master Marlowe must have something to do with the devil, for such bad luck to plague him," Sam insisted.

"When Faustus in the play sold his soul to the devil, it was for good fortune all his life," I countered. "Why should Master Marlowe, or anyone, deal with the devil if only to get ill luck in exchange?"

"Enough talk of this," Nat said firmly. "Master Henslowe would not like it. Leave it to the Puritans to say we are all devil worshippers. Need we denounce each other? Come. There's work to do before the performance begins."

Robin hung behind the other boys to walk beside me as we made our way back inside. "Sam's an old gossip," he said, glancing sideways at me. "Do not mind it. But *is* there anything?"

"Anything about what?"

"About Master Marlowe. 'Tis nothing, I am sure. Only they say. . . ."

"What, for mercy's sake?" Now Robin, too, was going to question me about my master? "What do they say?"

"Oh . . . things!" Robin shrugged helplessly as I turned to glare at him. "Nothing so much . . . only that he was a friend of Sir Walter Raleigh. And Raleigh went to the Tower."

Master Marlowe had friends of such high rank? I had not known it. Raleigh, once the queen's favorite, then condemned as a traitor, if for nothing more than marrying without her leave. . . .

"Well, he's out again now," I answered shortly.

"Aye. But . . ."

"*What?*"

"Oh, Ros—" I scowled ferociously at him. "Richard!" he corrected himself hastily. "I do not know all they say. I only wondered."

"I wonder, too," I said crisply. "I wonder thou hast time to learn anything here at the playhouse, if all the players do is gossip the day long." What on earth did they want to know from me, Sam and now Robin? I ran Master Marlowe's errands and brushed his clothes, but if he had any secrets, he was hardly likely to confide them in me.

And he did have secrets, that was plain. Else why had he sent me out of the room when Tom Watson had arrived?

Well, I had secrets, too. If I did not pry into his, perhaps he would respect mine.

"And Master Cowley?" I asked Robin, to turn the talk into another channel. "He is kind to thee?"

"Aye, he is." Robin grinned widely. "And Mistress

Cowley makes marchpane for the crackropes."

"Good, then." We were at the playhouse door by now, and Robin saw Master Cowley across the yard, struggling with an armful of wooden swords. He ran to help his master, and after piling the swords into his arms, Master Cowley gave him an approving smile and ruffled his hair with affection, then pointed toward the stage, where Master Henslowe stood watching Master Alleyn and Harry rehearse a scene.

Watching from the doorway, I suddenly felt as if a fishhook had lodged itself in my throat. Was it so easy for Robin? A bit of sweet almond paste and a fatherly smile, and he had found himself a new family.

I knew it was not fair, even as I thought it. Did I begrudge Robin a kind master and a welcoming home? But I felt as lost as I had on that first day in London. The playhouse was Robin's place, not mine. There were women who scrubbed the stage or sold nuts and beer during the performances, but every player and apprentice was a man or a boy. If they knew the truth of what I was, they would bar the door to me.

Robin had friends, and a kind master, and work that he loved. But I had only a master with something to hide, and secrets of my own.

chapter eight
SEPTEMBER 1592

Robin dropped his armful of wooden swords on the stage just as Harry, in a black wig and an extravagant gown of gold tissue over white brocade, swept his arms out and sank into a low curtsey. Half the swords missed the edge of the stage and fell to the ground with a clatter. Robin hopped back to save his toes and Harry lost his balance, stumbled forward, and trod heavily on the hem of his skirt. There was an ominous sound of stitches giving way as he straightened up.

I ran to help Robin pick up the swords, and Harry looked down in dismay. Several points, the tapes that tied the skirt to the bodice, had been ripped loose, and there was a gap at his waist, showing a patched shirt underneath the silk.

"Clumsy oaf!" Master Henslowe exclaimed, enraged. "Hast torn it?"

"'Twas his fault!" Harry insisted, pointing at Robin. "If he had not made such a noise—"

"Oh, indeed?" Master Henslowe snapped back. "And thinkst thou that, during a performance, thou'lt never hear anything to startle thee? A player keeps his lines in his head and his feet on the stage, no matter what befalls! And if thou canst not do that, thou'rt not fit for this part."

Harry's face flushed red and he scowled at the ground. "'Tis but a woman's part," he muttered. Perhaps he did not mean anyone to hear, but he was a player after all, and it came naturally to him to speak clearly on a stage.

I had been about the playhouse for less than a month, but even I knew better than to answer Master Henslowe in such a way. Hastily I helped Robin pile the rest of the swords back up on the stage and held my breath, waiting for the explosion.

But to my surprise, it did not come. "Master Henslowe," drawled a patient voice as Master Alleyn intervened. "You are welcome to beat the boy senseless after the performance. Indeed, I recommend it. But if you do so now, I will have no Zenocrate to make love to this afternoon. Pray, may we continue?"

Master Henslowe seemed to bubble with rage at Harry's impudence, but he recognized the truth of Master Alleyn's words. "Well, take it off then, take it off," he snapped at Harry, who began to fumble with the remaining points. "Thou canst rehearse in thy breeches, I hope? Or hast forgotten how to speak as well as how to walk? Mark well," he added venomously as he snatched the skirt from Harry's hands. "Pretty boys I can pick up by the dozen in the stews, but lace and brocade cost *money!*"

"I am sorry," Harry mumbled, standing shamefaced in his gorgeous bodice and shabby breeches.

"Sorry, aye, if thou'rt not now, thou wilt be after the performance is over. Here, boy." Master Henslowe threw the skirt in Robin's direction, but Robin's hands were full of the last few swords he'd picked up, so I caught the armful of gold and white before it could land on the ground. "Take it to the tireman and have it mended," Master Henslowe ordered. "From your speech, Master Alleyn, I pray you."

"This way," Robin said to me, and I followed him backstage and along a narrow passageway to a half-open door.

"Master Green," Robin said, sticking his head into the room. "Harry has torn his gown and it must be mended."

"Indeed?" said a dry, impatient voice. "And what else did Henslowe expect, putting a flat-footed lout like that into one of my best gowns? Bring it here; let me see the damage."

I went behind Robin into the room and drew in my breath.

It was little more than a closet, with one window in the far wall. But it was packed full to bursting with color. For an instant I was back in my father's warehouse, with the smell of wool and the rolls of cloth stacked up to the ceiling. But here there was more than wool. Chests lined the walls, and above them from hooks hung cloaks and skirts and hats and gowns and doublets in sea-blue velvet, grass-green satin, red silk and ivory lace and taffeta the yellow of sunlight. If a rainbow had come apart at the seams, it might have looked like this room.

Master Green, the tireman, was small and thin and stooped over from his work, with spectacles perched on his nose. He sat on a stool near the window, sewing a new sleeve onto a doublet of crimson velvet. "Well, let's see, then," he said, and I handed the skirt to him. "Not so bad, only a few points. Go and find Will and tell him to mend it. I must finish this doublet for Master Alleyn."

"Would not green suit him better?"

The words were out of my mouth before I realized that they might sound like a criticism. It had been the memory of Master Alleyn's face on stage that had prompted me to speak. He was dark-haired and red-cheeked, and his face flushed easily with emotion or heat. A crimson doublet would make him look parboiled.

Master Green's spectacles slid down his nose and he

looked at me in surprise. "And thy name is?"

"My brother, Richard," Robin said. "I'll go and find Will, then."

"Kit Marlowe's boy?" Although Robin's hand was out for the torn skirt, Master Green did not hand it to him, but only looked quizzically at me, as if marveling at the impudence of a servant.

"Pardon, master," I mumbled, ducking my head. Had I not just vowed to stay quiet and in the background? "I did not mean—"

"Quite right, green would suit him much better," Master Green said, waving his hand, still holding a needle, as if to brush my apology aside. "But he is to play Tamburlaine, a barbarian king, and it must be red, to show he is a bloodthirsty tyrant. So he will storm and sulk, but he must wear it. A ruff around the neck will help, to draw the red away from his face."

A white ruff against red? He would look like a clown. "Or a fur trim, perhaps?" I said thoughtfully, my mind caught up by the idea of color on color. "Like this." I was not sure what animal it had come from, but the fur I picked up from the top of a chest was a rich brown with undertones of gold.

Master Green took the fur from me and laid it across the red velvet on his lap. "Thou mayst be right." He held the combination up to the light. "Thou hast an eye for color, indeed. Go on, then, Robin, what art waiting for? Find Will and get that mended."

"I should have known better," I muttered to myself as I followed Robin back out of the tireroom. I had known far too much about clothes for a boy named Richard.

"He thought nothing of it," Robin said cheerfully. "Now, where's Will gotten himself to?"

"Robin, hurry!" Sam was suddenly at Robin's elbow. "Master Edmont is to give us a fencing lesson. Come, he's waiting."

"But I must find Will," Robin protested. "He's to mend this skirt of Harry's."

"I saw him go up into the second gallery," Sam said, pointing.

"Richard, wilt look for him?" Robin asked, turning to me. "Please? Master Edmont is the best fencer in the company, and 'tis rare that he teaches the crackropes."

"Hurry!" Sam called, running back toward the stage as Robin thrust the armful of skirt at me.

"But who is Will?" I asked helplessly.

"The 'prentice tireman," Robin called, already turning to follow Sam.

With no other choice, I tucked the skirt more securely into my arms and climbed the stairs to the galleries.

I saw no one in the second gallery and went on to the third, the highest. But that was empty, too. Frowning, I started back down. Sam must have been mistaken. But as I passed the second gallery, something caught my eye.

It was a shoe, lying upon one of the benches as though some player had carelessly abandoned it there. Except that there was a foot in this shoe, and a leg attached to the foot. A few steps nearer and I could see a boy, perhaps a year or two older than I was, lying flat on his back in the space between the first bench and the gallery railing, intent on a book he held open a few inches from his nose. It was a perfect hiding place. No one could see him from the stage below, and if he had not left a foot propped up on the bench, I would probably have missed him as well.

I cleared my throat. He did not move.

"Pardon. Are you Will?"

The boy sprang up as if he'd been stung by a bee, and his book almost flew over the railing into the midst of the fencing lesson below.

"I've finished. Nearly. A few stitches more. Who are *you*?"

With my arms full of cloth, I could not put my hands to my face to smother my smile. He was so quick to defend himself, and so startled to find that he was not being accused.

"Richard Archer," I introduced myself. "Robin's brother."

"Oh." He sighed with relief. "You nearly killed me with the shock. I thought you were come to hound me back to my work."

He brushed a length of bright yellow hair out of his eyes and grinned at me. The face that had been so studious a moment ago, and then so comically alarmed, was now friendly and cheerful.

"I was, I suppose. Master Green sent me to find you. This must be mended before the performance." There was the oddest pressure around my heart, as if someone had fixed an iron band about it, and was squeezing it gently but steadily tighter. I showed Will the torn points on Harry's skirt, hoping to draw his attention away from my face.

"Ah, God's teeth, *today's* performance?" Will looked wildly alarmed. "I'll never finish it! I was meant to be sewing these tabards for the soldiers. I thought I had time enough. . . ." He looked at a heap of red and yellow linen on the floor, a threaded needle stuck into the cloth, as if he expected it to have sewn itself up while he read.

"I could help," I offered. He blinked at me in surprise. "My father was a wool merchant"—this, at least, was true—"and a tailor as well"—this was not. "I have some skill with a needle." I fervently hoped Robin had said nothing to contradict my claim.

Will, however, was far too relieved to wonder. "Can you, truly? A miracle! If you can finish these tabards, I can do this skirt of Harry's. Half the points ripped off, and here's the lace at the hem torn, too. God's teeth, he's a clumsy ox, is he not? He's grown much too tall this past winter to play the women's parts. Sit you down here, Richard. I thank you a thousand times. You've saved me a beating from that slave driver, that sour-faced, short-sighted, mean-spirited wretch."

I was already spreading the first tabard, a simple smock with no sleeves, out on my knee to see what needed to be done. "But he—is your master, is he not?" Even after weeks among the folk of the playhouse, I was still a little shocked at the freedom of their tongues.

Will groaned as his long, thin fingers tugged at the points on Harry's skirt to see which would need repair. "Worse than that. He is my father. If I were only an apprentice, I might buy my freedom, but a son has no such escape."

I bit my lip and bent my head over my sewing. Three stitches, four, five.

"I am sorry, Richard. I had forgotten about your father."

"You know?"

"Of course. All the playhouse knows." He shrugged and smiled gently. "We spend so much time together, there are no secrets here. I beg pardon for speaking so carelessly."

He sounded honestly contrite. I gave him a quick smile, though it came hard, to show I bore no ill will. "You wish to escape?" I asked. "And where would you go?" Anything to take us away from the subject of fathers.

"Where? Anywhere!" He snatched up his book from the bench and waved it in my direction. "The Indies! The New World! They say there are cities of gold, and savages who eat men's hearts, and jungles with beasts no one has ever seen. And my father expects me to sit here in this prison, sewing players' rags all my life!" He jabbed the needle angrily into the white silk.

I finished one tabard and picked up another. Below us Master Alleyn's voice boomed from the stage.

> *"I hold the fates bound fast in iron chains,*
> *And with my hand turn Fortune's wheel*
>   *about,*
> *And sooner shall the sun fall from his sphere,*
> *Than Tamburlaine be slain or overcome."*

Magnificent, his rich voice rolling forth like a dark, deep river. Magnificent, but absurd. No one held the fates captive, no one spun Fortune's wheel at his own will. Not Tamburlaine the barbarian king nor Will the tireman's son. We were all who we had been born to be.

But I had not been born to be Richard, a playmaker's servant boy, and yet here I sat, in my breeches and doublet, sewing costumes in the playhouse, and no one suspected my duplicity. If my new life as Richard was so easy, what did that say of my old life as Rosalind? Was that the secret of the Rose—that none of our lives were any more real than a part played on Master Henslowe's stage?

We had been sewing quietly for some little time when Will spoke again, and now his voice was more wistful than angry. "They show foreign lands on that stage every day, and people crowd in to see it. But 'tis all a show, 'tis nothing. When there are *true* lands to explore, lands where no one has ever set foot, how could anyone be content to molder away here?" His gaze went up over the roofs of the galleries to the clear sky, though his hands never faltered in their quick, neat work.

I knew what it was to long for something like that, something beyond my reach. The iron band inside me loosened suddenly and, released from its pressure, my heart seemed to turn liquid and gush out into the hollow spaces of my chest. I wished I could speak, to tell Will that I understood a little of what he felt. But I was no playmaker like Master

Marlowe, no player like Master Alleyn, to let words roll easily and lightly off my tongue.

"You think it foolish, no doubt." His eyes were back on his sewing.

"No, in truth—"

"There, 'tis done." He bit the thread off deftly between his teeth. "Why, you're finished as well. You are wasted as a servant, Richard; you should find a place as a tailor's apprentice. I'll repay you for your help one day."

I thought to tell him there was no need of repayment, but he was already getting to his feet, folding the tabards neatly and setting the skirt on top. Then he held out a hand to me.

"Many thanks, Richard."

His skin was smooth and warm.

"I hope you get your wish, Will Green," I said to him. His eyes were blue, like cornflowers wet with rain. He looked a little puzzled at my earnestness, as well he might, and I blushed suddenly, my cheeks painfully hot. What must he be thinking? I tugged my hand free, muttered a graceless farewell, and hurried down the gallery stairs.

How could I have forgotten, even for a moment, that I was no longer Rosalind? That Will Green saw a servant boy when he looked at me, and a fool of one at that? Did I think I could hide a woman's heart under a man's doublet?

Did I think I could keep up this lie when convenient, and discard it when I chose?

I scolded myself all the way back to Master Marlowe's lodgings. It was better than crying in the streets.

chapter nine
SEPTEMBER 1592

❧

Not many days after my first meeting with Will, I woke in the night to find that I'd drunk too much with dinner. Now the ale was making itself felt. There was a chamber pot, of course, but to use it was out of the question. If Master Marlowe were to wake and find me crouching rather than standing over the pot, it would be the end of all my concealment.

The nights had taken on a touch of real chill, and I lay for some time with the blanket clutched to my chin before I gave up and admitted that I must slip outside to the privy, or I would never be able to sleep for the rest of the night.

All was dark and quiet in Master Marlowe's room. As was usual, he had not come home by the time I'd gone to bed. But it was pitch black outside now, and the streets were silent. Even Master Marlowe would not be abroad this late. He must have come in while I was sleeping. Moving quietly so as not to wake him, I pulled on my breeches, carried my shoes until I could sit on the stairs to put them on, and dashed to the privy in the yard to take care of my needs.

Back inside, I was preparing to climb the stairs when the front door to the shop shifted slightly as if touched by a breeze. It had been left unlatched.

Master Marlowe was usually the last one in at night. He must have carelessly forgotten to lock the door behind him. I went to do it myself, but paused as I heard the mutter of voices close by, as if men were standing on the doorstep. Thieves! My hand darted to fasten the latch and shut them out, but then I recognized the voice that was speaking.

"I've no time for it now. I've a new play to finish."

It was Master Marlowe.

"Shall I tell the hunchback so?" The other man had a smooth, gentle voice, tender as a woman's.

"What's the need for it, Pooley?" I had never heard Master Marlowe sound like this—exhausted, humble, almost pleading. "We burned the Spanish ships on the sea, and France is half our friend. Who is there that threatens us now? And I've work to do."

"What a poor fool of a poet you are after all, Kit." That

soft voice should have been soothing to listen to, but somehow it was not. It sounded as if the speaker knew a secret that made a mock of the rest of the world. "Did you think you could leave the hunchback's service any time you chose?"

"I have other men will speak for me," Master Marlowe said sharply. The second man laughed.

"Do you think your highborn friend will save you? Poor, fond Kit. Dedicate your poems to him by all means, but do not trust him to keep you from having your conscience scraped clean if you cross the hunchback's will. Look here." Through the crack between the door and the frame, I could see the dim glow of a horn lantern. "My master did that to me, stretched me on the rack just to find out what I knew. And I was working for him at the time, mind you."

"I thought you were working for the Queen of Scots," Master Marlowe said coldly.

I had backed away from the door as quietly as I could, thinking to creep up the stairs so that Master Marlowe would not catch me listening to his conversation. But at this sentence I froze in shock.

Mary, Queen of Scots, Elizabeth's cousin Mary, who was a Catholic? They said she had plotted against Elizabeth's crown and her life. But was it true? True enough, at any rate, that Elizabeth had executed her for it.

And Master Marlowe, who was a friend of Sir Walter Raleigh's, just out of the Tower—he knew a man who'd worked for her?

Pooley laughed, as if it were a joke to hear himself all but accused of treason.

"Ah, well, it was one of them," he answered lightly. "Perhaps even both. You are always working for someone in this business, Kit, do not forget. I'll speak with you soon." His voice grew fainter as if he were walking away.

The door swung inward. The light from the lantern in Master Marlowe's hand fell on me.

Shock held us both transfixed for the space of a heartbeat. Then, before I could move or speak, Master Marlowe had dropped the lantern, which went out as it hit the ground, took three steps inside, and had one hand clamped around my arm. There was the faint silky whisper of sharpened metal sliding from a sheath.

"What dost mean, overlistening our speech?" His voice was rough and low, full of menace. A variety of noises tumbled out of my throat, none of them quite full-blown words, but all meant to convince him of my innocence and harmlessness. In the distance I heard the call of the watch: "One o'clock and all's well!" All was not in the least well, since I seemed likely to lose my place and my home, if not my head, in the next few moments.

Master Marlowe heard the watchman's call, too. He let his rapier slide back into its sheath. Still holding me fast by the arm, he kicked the door shut behind him, latched it, bent down to snatch up the lantern, and pushed me ahead of him up the narrow staircase, all without a word.

Once in his lodgings, he let me go, but he still did not speak, not until he had shut the door and struck a spark to light the lantern again. Then he turned to face me. I was still shivering in my thin shirt from the chill of the night air, rubbing my arm where his fingers had bruised and wrenched it, sick to my stomach and waiting for disaster, wrath, and ruin to fall. Would he at least let me stay until morning? Or would he cast me out into the London night, prey for every thief and worse? Would he let me take the few things I owned—the old doublet, my purse with its pitiful few shillings?

Master Marlowe reached out a hand toward me. I flinched, expecting a blow, but he only passed the backs of his fingers quickly across my cheek, a touch that was almost gentle. His thumb lingered a moment under my jaw. Before I could understand what his action meant, he frowned and pushed me so that I stumbled back a pace or two away from him.

"Did they send thee to spy on me?" Master Marlowe

demanded. In the tarnished light that shone through the sheets of horn shielding the lantern's flame, his face looked savage, thinner and older. "Are they watching me? Who hired thee?"

I could only gape wordlessly in confusion.

"Thou'rt not—what I thought thee." His hand fell to his sword hilt again. "*Whose art thou?*"

I held out my empty hands to show him I was unarmed, defenseless, helpless. "No one's, master, I swear it. I serve you only. I do not understand," I pleaded. I had thought him mad the first time I'd met him, but with a light, bantering lunacy. Not like this. This was a madness with a rapier's edge. This was a man who wrote verse about bloody murder.

"I found thee in the street," Master Marlowe said, eyeing me strangely. "They could not know I'd pick thee up out of the gutter. But they might have hired thee since."

"No one has hired me, master. No one but you." I felt the weakness of it, and longed for some kind of proof. The truth felt flimsy as a cobweb next to the fire of his suspicion. "I will swear it. I will swear by anything."

A look of cunning touched Master Marlowe's face, and suddenly he took two long steps to kneel down by my bed and reach beneath the pallet. He stood again to face me, with my rosary dangling from his fingers.

"Wilt swear by thy saints?"

A gasp froze into a block of ice in my throat. A tiny piece of my brain thought gratefully that at least he'd missed the linen wrappings, but this was bad enough.

Master Marlowe smiled briefly, showing his teeth. "Didst think I did not know? That I do not recognize Latin when I hear it? I've been in Newgate, Richard. There are few debtors there. But a goodly number of papists." He flung the rosary at me and I fumbled to catch it. "Thou'rt a clumsy liar. Indeed, 'tis why I half believe thee now. But swear it."

"Master, please," I whispered. "Do not denounce me."

"I care not if thou prayest in Latin or English or a heathen tongue of the Indies," Master Marlowe said impatiently. "Thy soul is none of my concern. But thou believest, I know. Let me hear thee swear on thy saints that thou art no spy."

Was it a trap? Did he only want to hear me swear by a Catholic saint so that he could accuse me and see me tossed, along with my brother, into the prison that had killed my father? But he stood between me and the door, and his hand was still on his sword. I knew if I did not satisfy him now, it was not just my place I was in danger of losing.

"By the Holy Virgin and Saint Anne her mother, I

swear it," I choked out, my voice shaking over the oath. "As I shall be saved, I am no spy."

Suddenly he moved toward me, his hand reaching for my throat. I gasped, but he only seized my jaw between his fingers and strained my head back so that he could look into my eyes. I am sure he saw nothing but terror there, and it seemed enough for him. He let his breath out in a long, slow sigh.

"Well, I will believe thee. For tonight." His hand moved quickly, and he had my ear pinched between two fingers, pulling hard enough that I thought it would come out at the roots. I rose up on my toes, trying to ease the pressure, but he only pulled the harder.

"Listen well, now. It would be better for thee that I slice this ear off than that thou shouldst remember what took place tonight. Forget it, Richard." Strangely, his voice was no longer angry. He sounded only grieved and very tired, even as he gave my ear such a cruel twist that I could not hold back a whimper. "Thou'rt afraid? Be so. 'Tis for thine own good I speak it. Better to have stayed on the streets where I found thee, than come to know too much of my affairs. Dost understand?"

Of course, I said that I did. I would have said anything by then, to make him let go. He did so. I clapped a hand over my throbbing ear.

"What wast thou doing downstairs in the black of night?"

"The privy, master," I said as humbly as I could.

He snorted. "God's teeth. Next time piss in a pot and spare both of us." And, turning, he snatched up the lantern from the table. It swung in his hand and made black shadows flail and flare wildly across the walls and ceiling as he strode to his bedchamber. The light disappeared when he shut the door behind him.

"Thou shouldst leave his service," Robin said the next morning.

"How can I?" I asked despondently. "I've a contract with him for a year."

"But even so—if he knows the truth—"

We sat backstage at the Rose, tucked into a dark corner where we hoped no one would overhear.

"No one would take me for a servant if I've broken my last contract," I pointed out. "And I've hardly any money, Robin." Quarter day, when I'd be paid the first of my wages, had not yet come.

"Thou couldst change thy name again. He would not follow thee."

"He'd have no need to." Robin frowned in confusion. "Dost not see? If he knows I am . . ." I could not say it aloud. "If he knows the truth about me, he knows it about thee as well."

Robin looked startled, and then ill.

"As long as thou'rt here, Master Marlowe would have no need to pursue me across London. He knows I would not go far from thee. And I do not suppose thou'lt leave the playhouse even now."

"'Tis my *place*," he muttered awkwardly. "I've nowhere else—"

"Nor I."

"But he has known—and for long?"

"I know not. Since early on, I think." He'd known my lie for what it was, when I said that our father was in Newgate for debt. That must have aroused his suspicions, and then my carelessness had let him catch a whispered prayer and glimpse the rosary tucked beneath my pallet.

"And he has not told. So perhaps . . ."

"Aye, but we do not know *why* he has not—"

"Good day, Will!"

My nerves were so bad that I jumped like a startled cat. Will, standing behind me with a tangle of old hose in his hands and a red doublet over his arm, gave me a puzzled look.

"They want you onstage," he said to Robin. "Good day, Richard. Are you well?"

"We'll talk more on't later," I said to Robin as we got to our feet, and he gave me an anxious look as he hurried off toward the stage.

"What's the trouble?" Will asked.

"'Tis nothing."

"Oh, indeed? I thought the Spanish had invaded, from your look. Come, truly, what is wrong?"

I hesitated. But he could see from my face that I was worried, and he seemed honestly concerned. Almost as if I were a friend.

"My master's angry with me," I said, dancing awkwardly around the truth. *Thou'rt a clumsy liar,* Master Marlowe had said to me last night, and I feared he was right. "I overheard him last night, speaking to a man. 'Twas an accident, in truth, but he seemed so . . ."

"Did he beat you?" Will asked sympathetically.

"No." He had only drawn his sword on me, that was all.

"Well, then, his wrath cannot have been much," Will said cheerfully. "My father's angry with me twice a day at least, but it comes to nothing. Bruises mend, after all."

"And what dost thou backstage?"

Will jumped almost as badly as I had done to find his father at his elbow. Master Green frowned at his son over his spectacles.

"Master Cowley sent me to find Robin Archer," Will said in quick defense.

"And if thou hadst been in the tireroom at thy work, Master Cowley would not have sent thee to run his errands," Master Green said severely. "Hast Master Alleyn's doublet there? Look here, Richard." Will handed the doublet to his father and Master Green shook it by the shoulders, holding it out so that I could see. "It looks well, does't not? The fur was an excellent thought."

It did look well, the red and golden brown just as I had imagined them, rich and grand and a little savage, well suited to a barbarian king.

"Aye, Richard, well done," Will said. "I'll take these hose up to the galleries and mend them."

"No, thou wilt not!" Master Green's voice, friendly and approving before, was suddenly harsh. "Thou canst work well enough in the tireroom. Thou hast no need to idle away thy time watching the players." He strode toward the stage, leaving Will with a face as sullen and threatening as a thundercloud.

"Did he discover it?" I asked tentatively. "That you were reading that day?"

"No, he did not!" Will was scowling in the direction his father had taken. "No, thanks to you, he never knew I'd been idling away my time." Even in his anger, he remembered to give me a grateful smile. "What harm if I sit and sew in the galleries, where I can see the sun, instead of in that dark pit? 'Tis only his ill nature."

Master Green had not been ill-natured toward me, I thought in confusion. He had even been kind. But when his attention had turned to his son . . .

"Enough," Will said. "Come, Richard, I've an idea."

We passed by the tireroom, where Will tossed the hose inside, and out into the yard below the stage. "But your father," I protested. "And my master . . ."

"Your master is shut up with Henslowe; they'll be an age at the least. And Master Alleyn will surely keep my father for an hour, fussing over the fit of that doublet. If he did not eat so much marchpane, he would not need to worry." Will glanced around warily before turning back to me. "Have you ever tried tobacco, Richard?"

"Tobacco? No." I'd heard of the plant, of course, a discovery from the New World, and I knew that in London people gathered in shops and taverns to puff on pipes full of the dried weed, but my village had been much too small and old-fashioned for anything so newfangled.

"Come, then," Will said, all his sulkiness gone, grinning with mischief. "Hurry!" And he set off at a run, dodging around players and hirelings and apprentices.

There was no excuse for it, I knew. Will should have

been at his work and my master had not given me leave to go gallivanting about London. No excuse, except that since I'd come to London with the ruins of my old life behind me, I had been grieved and lonely and anxious and frightened nearly to death, but never so close to happy as I was then, running out of the playhouse and into the clear autumn sunlight, following Will Green.

chapter ten
SEPTEMBER 1592

Will took me to a small shop a few streets away from the
Rose. The smell of the place tickled the back of my throat.
It was like woodsmoke and crushed nuts, a little sweet, a
little harsh.

"Enough to fill my pipe, Master Spence, please," Will
said to the owner, a tall, gloomy-looking man with hollow
cheeks and a rough voice, as though he had a cold. "And
my friend has no pipe of his own. Can you lend him one,
and we'll buy enough tobacco to fill it?"

But I touched Will's sleeve, feeling a blush fan out
across my cheeks. "I have—" I had to clear my throat and
start again. "I have no money. I'm sorry, Will."

Will looked surprised. "Nay, I would not let you pay in
any case. 'Tis my thanks for your help a few days ago." I
protested a little, feebly, for Will was only an apprentice
and had no money to throw away on gifts, but he did not

heed. He paid three pence for each of us. Master Spence lit our pipes with a coal held in a pair of tongs, and Will carried them outside to a bench where we could sit in the sunlight.

Will showed me how to take the pipe between my teeth and draw in the smoke with my breath. I did as he said, but my first try made me feel as if I were choking.

Will laughed and held my pipe for me while I gasped for air. "'Tis always so, the first time," he reassured me. "But 'tis very good for the lungs, tobacco. It cures all sorts of ailments. Look!" And he breathed out twin streams of white smoke from his nostrils.

"Like a dragon," I said, and drew in another careful breath. This time I did not cough, and sighed the smoke back out, watching it drift away on the breeze. Tobacco must loosen the tongue like wine, for before I realized it, I was telling Will the most peculiar thing of all about last night: how Master Marlowe seemed to have forgotten the whole thing by the morning.

"Well, that's good, if he is no longer angry," Will said practically.

"But 'twas so strange. He made a jest about the weather. . . ." If there had not been five purple marks on my arm, left there by Master Marlowe's fingers, I might have thought that some spirit had settled on my chest last night and breathed a nightmare into me. But dreams do not leave bruises.

"Perhaps he was drunk," Will offered. "Or it may be 'twas a moneylender he spoke to, or a bawd. Something he's ashamed to have known. 'Twould be best if you pretended to forget."

It was honest advice, and well meant, and I'd been foolish to speak of my worries in any case, when I could not say what was worrying me most. I could not tell Will of my own secret, the one Master Marlowe knew.

Perhaps Robin was right. Perhaps I should leave his service after all, simply walk back out into the London streets and be free of this tangle of players and playmakers, secrets and lies and things I was not meant to know. Though there was danger in going—How would I find work? Where would I sleep?—there was danger in staying as well. Master Marlowe knew what faith I cherished. At any moment he might betray me.

But he had known for weeks, or so he claimed. If he planned to hand me over to the law, why had he not done so already?

"Nay, be off! I'll serve none of thy kind here!"

I nearly dropped my pipe at the shout. Master Spence's rough, deep voice, when raised, was as formidable as Master Henslowe's. Peering into the shop, I could only see the back of a tall, fair-haired man standing before the counter, but he seemed ordinary and inoffensive enough. His voice, when it drifted out to us, had a heavy accent that sounded familiar. He spoke like Mistress Pieters and the man I'd seen in her shop. He must have been a Dutchman.

"I only want tobacco, nothing more. See, I can pay—"

"Oh, thou canst pay, I've no doubt! All thy kind are rich enough, taking bread from the mouths of honest men born and raised here. Go on, out of my shop!" Master Spence might have added more harsh words if he had not been interrupted by a fit of coughing, and so the stranger managed to depart without his tobacco, but with some dignity still.

But he was not five paces into the street when a fist-sized glob of mud, thrown from no one could tell where, splattered itself across the shoulder of his fine broadcloth doublet. Then, as he spun around to find the source of the missile, another hit the back of his head. This perhaps had a stone in it, for the man gave a sharp cry of pain.

"Foreign bastard!" shouted a voice, and the man turned again, one hand to his head. Was there red mixed with the brown mud that oozed through his fingers?

"How dost like thine own filth?" another voice demanded. There were five men across the narrow street from Master Spence's shop. They were older than Will, but young enough to wear the blue doublets and flat wool caps of apprentices. One held a heavy stick in his hand. The others clustered behind him.

"I have done nothing!" the man shouted.

Beside me, Will groaned softly. "'Sblood, man, just run," he muttered under his breath.

Laying my borrowed pipe down on the bench, I glanced around for help, but the passersby only slowed to watch with interest or hurried on their way. Master Spence, leaning in the doorway of his shop, looked on with satisfaction.

"Aye, nothing but take work from Englishmen!" the young man with the stick shouted back. More mud flew. The foreigner put up a hand to shield his face and took a pace or two toward his tormentors.

"Aye, come and greet us, Dutchman!"

"A friendly welcome to England!"

"Leave him be, you were best!"

It was Will's voice, shouting. He was on his feet, fists clenched. The boys turned toward us, and I felt the shock of their malice from across the street. I wanted to shrink back, as from the snap of a whip.

"Aye, art thou one too?" the oldest apprentice sneered. Mud splattered on the wall of Master Spence's shop, just over Will's shoulder.

"Damnation, boy, get away from my shop if thou must interfere in such a thing as this!" Master Spence snapped, pushing Will a step or two forward into the street, so that he stood beside the beleaguered foreigner.

The oldest apprentice lifted his stick. The foreign man laid a hand on the hilt of his dagger. Will tightened his fists.

"The Lord Mayor! I see him!"

It was absolutely ridiculous, of course, but it was the only thing I could think of to do or say. I pointed to the alleyway behind the apprentice boys. Without thinking, they turned to look. Will clapped a hand on the stranger's shoulder and hissed, "Run!" The man, belatedly, took to his heels down an alleyway. Two of the apprentices went after him. Before the other three could make up their minds who they hated more, the foreigner or his defenders, Will and I were running in the opposite direction.

Will's legs were longer than mine, but I made up the difference in sheer terror, and kept right by his side as we skidded over cobbles and scrambled around corners. I slipped on a pile of rotting straw, but Will caught my arm and hauled me around the next corner more by his strength than my own. Then it was a straight dash for the doorway of the Rose and safety.

Or it would have been safety, had we reached it.

I was running as fast as I could, when Will suddenly vanished from my side. Later I learned that one of the apprentices had thrown a stick that tangled in his feet and tripped him up. At the time I only knew that he was suddenly gone, and I looked back to see him sprawled full length on the cobblestones.

I did not stop to think that the Rose was perhaps ten yards behind me, or that I was only a girl, no match in height or breadth for the young man who had just kicked Will in the ribs, or the other two ready to join in. I certainly did not pause to consider that brawling in the streets was nothing Rosalind Archer would ever have done.

I hit, I kicked—I think it is possible that I may have bitten one of them. Rage gave me, if not strength, then at least determination. How dared these ruffians, these brawlers, these layabouts who should have been at their work—how dared they set upon Will, three against one? How dared they attack a friendless stranger who had done them no harm? Just as my father had done no harm, and I myself as well. Why should we be forced to walk the streets in fear, never free to be ourselves in safety?

Unfortunately, rage did not give me any skill at fighting, and Will, already bruised and breathless from his fall, was getting the worst of things himself and unable to aid me. A blow knocked me flat on my back on the cobbles. There was a glint of metal, a flash in my eyes against the bright blue sky. I threw up a hand, palm out, fingers wide, to ward off the blow, and felt a pain, sharp and stinging, as if I'd tried to catch hold of a handful of broken glass.

Then my attacker fell back with a startled cry, and I sat up, bewildered. Sander was standing over me with his fists clenched. Nat and Sam were busy hauling Will's assailant off him, and Robin was running full tilt to help. And Harry—Harry, of all people, proud, sullen Harry who disdained to keep company with the other crackropes— Harry held the third, oldest apprentice at bay with a rapier at his throat.

Of course, it was only a stage weapon, blunt as an old pen. But it *looked* real enough. The boy was going crosseyed, trying to see the point an inch below his chin.

"Begone and stay gone," said Harry in his player's voice, soft and elegantly threatening but still pitched to reach the ears of the other two apprentices. "Three on two, is't, and one of the two no more than half-sized? There's courage, indeed. Keep away from the playhouse in the future, or I'll not be so generous." And he lowered his weapon a few inches.

"Playhouse scum!" the young man spat, too angry to

think clearly about who held the sword.

Harry's rapier flicked up to stop an inch from his eye. One of the other apprentices clambered up from the pavement where Sander had thrown him, took one look at Harry, and fled. Sam and Nat shoved the other after him, and Harry's opponent scowled but turned slowly, with an air of contempt, to go.

When Harry slashed the rapier like a whip across his backside, however, he went a bit more quickly.

Will sat up, laughing and wincing, with a hand to his ribs. "Well, what kept you? Richard and I were doing well enough on our own, of course, but—Richard?"

I was sitting stock still, looking in fascination and horror at my right hand.

My attacker must have held a knife. That was what I had seen, sharp and bright against the sky. It had cut a slash all the way across my palm, deep and spilling bright red blood freely over my breeches and the muddy cobblestones.

My right hand. My writing hand.

There was a good deal of confusion. I remember Robin steadying me with his arm around my waist and walking me toward the playhouse door. I remember John the porter bellowing for Master Henslowe, and Master Green shaking his son angrily by the shoulder as Will tried to explain what had happened. Master Alleyn, in his new red doublet with the fur trim, was frowning to have rehearsal interrupted. But Master Marlowe spoke no word to add to the din. He simply laid a hand on my shoulder and steered me, with Master Green following, down the street to a surgeon.

A man was leaving the surgeon's as we came in, supported between two friends, groaning, clutching a cloth stained with crimson to his mouth, and looking ill indeed.

"That tooth did not wish to come out of his jaw," said a plump man cheerfully, coming forward as he wiped the blood from his hands. "Perhaps he should have let it rot a few more days. Now what is to do here?"

I did my best not to scream while my hand was stitched back together, salved, and bandaged. After I had drunk a cup of willow bark tea, which helped to settle my stomach, though it did little for the pain in my hand, the surgeon declared that it was fortunate the wound was a clean cut and easily stitched, that I should do very well, and that if any in our party wished for a haircut or a shave, he would be delighted to oblige.

"Not today, I thank you," Master Marlowe said, eyeing the man's blood-stained fingers with distaste. "And he'll be able to use the hand again?"

"Assuredly," the surgeon promised. "Of course, if you

had taken him to a less skillful surgeon, it might have been most serious. But happily, sirs, I have the highest training."

"Happily," Master Marlowe agreed dryly, paying the man's fee. I winced to see so much silver change hands.

Master Green had watched silently as my hand was treated. Now he came forward. "I am sorry, Master Marlowe, for my son's part in what happened here," he said quietly, in a tone that boded no good for Will.

"'Twas not Will's fault, sir," I said quickly. I could not bear the thought of Will in yet more trouble with his father over me. "Without his help, that poor Dutchman would surely have been beaten, even killed. He was brave. . . ." I felt a blush creep up my cheeks and bit off the rest of my words. Perhaps it looked odd for Richard to praise Will so lavishly.

"He should have been at his work, not out in the streets," Master Green said gruffly.

"And I can still write, I am sure of it," I added to Master Marlowe. "In a day or so my hand will be as good as new."

Master Marlowe lifted one eyebrow skeptically, as if he could tell that my hand, stiff with bandages and throbbing with every heartbeat, felt as if it would never be as good as new again. But all he said, and that mildly, was, "Get thee home, Richard."

I made my way slowly over the bridge and back toward

Bishopsgate, cradling my right hand tenderly in my left to spare it any jolts, wondering bleakly what I would do if Master Marlow dismissed me out of hand. Then I smiled a little giddily at the thought, since I was out of hand myself.

But, truly, it was nothing to smile over. I'd had no leave to be out in the streets, I'd cost my master money, and I'd made myself useless for his service—and all this the day after he'd caught me listening to something he clearly did not want overheard. Was it too much to hope of mercy that he would keep me on?

An hour ago, I'd thought, and with relief, of leaving Master Marlowe. But now, half crippled as I was, how would I find a new place? Would I end up like the one-eyed, one-handed beggar of St. Paul's churchyard, grateful for stale crusts of bread from strangers?

Brooding over these matters, I paid little heed to my surroundings as I made my way over the bridge and up Fish Street. I did not notice the man hurrying in the other direction until he knocked against me, nearly sending me into the gutter. I gasped as the impact jarred my hand painfully. And when the man seized hold of my arm, in just the same place Master Marlowe had grasped it the night before, I could not hold back a cry of pain and alarm.

"Thou'rt Kit Marlowe's boy, art not?" the man said, glaring at me.

My heart settled back down in my chest. It was Master Marlowe's friend Tom Watson. I had not recognized him at first, since he looked so different from the last time I had seen him. Then he had been eager and lively, bursting with his news. Now his face was worn, as if he were ill or had not slept all night. His ruff, crisp and white before, was limp and gray, his hat gone.

"Give this to Kit," he said, pulling out a folded letter from inside his doublet. "And do not—" His hand closed hard around my arm. "*Do not read it,*" he said savagely. "I know thou'rt lettered. Keep thine eyes from other men's affairs." I was too startled to do more than nod. He released his hold on me and in an instant was gone into the crowd; I could not see what had become of him.

Awkwardly, using my left hand, I thrust the letter inside my doublet and went on. Strange friends Master Marlowe had. Had Master Watson been drunk, even though the bells had just struck three? It was the only reason I could think of for his odd behavior, and yet it did not quite satisfy me. He had not seemed himself, but not drunk, not precisely. He had seemed anxious, worried, uncertain of what to do. He had seemed . . . afraid.

What did he have to fear?

The words I'd heard the night before, spoken in the man Pooley's tender voice, rang in my head. *What a poor fool of a poet you are after all, Kit. . . . do not trust him to keep you from having your conscience scraped clean. . . .* That was what the queen's servants called the rack, and the manacles, and the fire. That was the way they scraped a man's conscience clean, found out everything he knew.

It was what they did to Catholics.

It was what they may have done to my father.

Once I had wondered if Master Marlowe was a secret Catholic himself. But no. Not the man who had flung my rosary at me with such contempt last night.

What else could my master be a part of, that he had the queen's torturers to fear? And what had driven his friend to the streets, looking as if something—or someone—were hunting him down?

Best not to know, I decided firmly. Best not to even wonder. I was bound to serve my master for a year, and now, with my right hand useless, I had very little chance of finding a place elsewhere. I could only hope that Master Marlowe had forgotten his anger of last night, that he would forgive my carelessness of today, and that he would keep me on.

In eleven months my contract would be over. By then my hand would be healed, I'd have my wages in my purse, and I would leave the playmaker's service for good. Perhaps—and even in my pain the thought of Will Green brought a blush to my cheeks—perhaps I could find a place where I could leave behind my breeches and doublet and be Rosalind again.

Until that time I would do as Master Marlowe, and Master Watson, and even Will had told me—shut my eyes, stop my ears, and pay no heed to Christopher Marlowe's affairs.

Mistress Stavesly took one look at my hand and another at my face and ordered me upstairs to bed. Some minutes later she brought me a cup of burnt wine, which she said would do more for the pain than all the willow bark tea in the world. It was harsh to the taste and seemed to scorch the back of my throat, but it did indeed help the pain, for it sent me straight to sleep.

I do not know how much later it was when I was roused by the sound of Master Marlowe's footsteps on the stairs. I sat up on my pallet as he came in, struggling clumsily with the blanket that seemed to have tangled itself around my legs.

Master Marlowe had not spoken, even to greet me. I might have thought his manner odd as he stood by the door, looking as if the room were unfamiliar to him. But my wits were still muddled by wine and sleep, and I thought of little but my message.

"Sir, there is a letter." My tongue felt thick and dry, as though a furry coating had grown on it while I had slept. I pointed with my uninjured hand. "There, on the table."

Still without speaking, Master Marlowe took up the letter. He turned it over in his hands, touching the broken seal with careful fingers, before he unfolded the paper. A moment later he was crouching by my pallet to look me in the face.

"Who gave thee this?" he demanded. "Who was it?" When I only blinked at him, startled and sleepy, he seized hold of my shoulder. "Richard, wake up. Who gave this to thee?"

"Your friend, sir," I said, working my tongue loose. "Tom Watson." I waited for more questions, but Master Marlowe only sat back on his heels, staring at the letter in his hand. I noticed, for the first time, a dark brown stain the size of a shilling on the top right corner of the paper.

I should have remembered my recent vow to pay no heed, to shut my eyes and ears. But my master looked as though he'd just been stabbed and was waiting now to die.

"Is all well, sir?"

Master Marlowe seemed to find he was not dying after

all. He folded the paper quickly, smoothing the creases with his long, ink-stained fingers. "Well enough with me," he answered, getting to his feet. "But not at all well with Tom. He's dead."

chapter eleven
september-
october 1592

When Master Marlowe arose the next morning, he found me sitting at the table, struggling to write with a hand that was stiff with bandages and dried blood and starting to ache with a tender pain that told of infection beginning. I had already burned the sheet of paper I'd ruined by trying to write with my left hand. With a sigh, Master Marlowe leaned over my shoulder to take the pen away from me.

"Richard," he said wearily. "Do not waste my good paper, please."

I slipped off the stool to stand respectfully, biting my lip as I looked at the awkward, straggling, uneven lines I'd taken such pains with, lines that would do no credit to a child of seven years. "I am sure my hand will heal in a few days' time, sir," I said hopefully.

Master Marlowe snorted, crumpled up the sheet of paper, and tossed it toward the fireplace. "Thou'rt sure?

Art now a surgeon as well as a scribe?"

I held my breath. Had I reached the end of his patience at last? Would he tell me to take my pitifully thin purse and go?

Master Marlowe seemed to guess what I was thinking. "If I'd been of a mind to turn thee out, Richard, I'd have done it two nights ago," he said impatiently. "Thou needst not fear losing thy place." He sat down heavily on the stool I had left empty and placed both elbows on the table, running his hands through his hair.

"Should I fetch breakfast, sir?" I suggested. I could manage ale and bread with my left hand.

"I've no stomach for it." He sighed, and I remembered, belatedly, that his friend was dead. "Fetch me some sack, Richard, from the tavern." I did not mean him to catch my quick glance at the sun on the windowsill. It still lacked some hours until noon. But he did see it, and frowned. "And none of thy papist looks," he said, suddenly angry. "Between a papist and a Puritan, indeed, there is not much to choose for pinch-lipped, prune-faced hypocrisy. . . ." But I was already scrambling out of the room and down the stairs, lest he take a mind to go on talking like this where somebody else could hear him.

When I came back with the wine, steaming hot and heavily sugared, he was sitting exactly as I had left him. He hardly stirred as I put the tankard at his elbow.

"Sir? Master Marlowe?" He glanced sideways at me, so I knew he was aware of my presence. My first instinct was to let him be, but he had been kind to me when my father died. I owed him something, now that death had touched his own life.

"Sir, I am sorry for his death," I said clumsily. "I am sorry, sir, for your friend."

"Thou'rt one of few, then," he said gloomily.

I should have left him, but something kept me there. Perhaps it was only a ghoul's curiosity, the kind that will keep people standing in a circle three deep around a duel or a public hanging.

"Was it an accident, sir?" Master Marlowe had not given me any more details, indeed, any more words, yesterday. And since the pain in my hand had kept me awake, I could not help wondering what had happened to Tom Watson. Had he been stuck by a cart or a wagon? Had it been something bloodier—a fight in a tavern, a blow given in wrath? A thief with a knife or a garrote in the dark?

"The plague, 'tis said." Master Marlowe took a long swallow of his sweet wine, but when he heard me gasp, he glanced at me in surprise over the rim of the tankard.

My hands were at my mouth. I had spoken to Tom

Watson. We had breathed the same air. He had certainly looked strange, not himself—had it been illness that had made him look so pale? And suddenly, in a whirl of fear, I remembered that libel pasted up on the playhouse wall—PLAYS CAUSE PLAGUE—and thought that perhaps I'd brought this on myself, spending time at a playhouse, consorting with players and tiremen and . . .

Master Marlowe wiped his mouth with the back of his hand and burst out laughing.

It was brief and not particularly merry. "Never fear, Richard," he said when he had finished. "If thou keepst thy wits about thee, thou needst have no fear of catching what Tom Watson died of."

That afternoon I peeled an onion and left it by my bed, to absorb any pestilential vapors. It was best to err on the safe side. But even before Master Marlowe laughed at my fears, I'd had enough time to realize my mistake, and to remember that a man dying of the plague would not be wandering the streets of London, looking no worse than drunk. Or deathly afraid.

The nights were cold in earnest, and by the time my hand had healed enough to let me write again, the darkness had nibbled away much of the afternoon light. The first task Master Marlowe set me was to make a clean copy of *The*

Massacre at Paris for him to deliver to the playhouse.

It gave me no joy to write out that play, and Master Marlowe knew it. Since the day after Tom Watson's death, he had made no mention of my religion. But there was the slightest mocking glint in his eye as he handed me the stack of pages, scrawled all over in his ragged black script, that showed me he had not forgotten.

If he expected objections or argument, he was disappointed. I set myself to the work without a word, thinking grimly that this was part of the bargain I had made— wages and food and a warm place to sleep in return for a year's silence. So I ground my teeth and copied out scene after scene where Catholics were traitors and murderers and the streets of Paris ran with innocent Protestant blood.

Most days Master Marlowe would go out on his own affairs. But on the day I was writing the final scene, he stayed, sitting by the fire. "This play will make a new name for me," he said as I dipped my pen in the ink. "And a new name is a new world."

There was a tankard of sack on the floor beside his stool, steaming slightly in the chill air. Perhaps that had loosened his tongue, for he spoke idly, lazily, as if hardly aware that I was listening.

He leaned against the wall, stretching out his feet

toward the hearth, and began to trim his fingernails with the ivory penknife. "A new world," he said thoughtfully, more to himself than me. "They sail off and discover new lands, dripping with jewels and pearls, and that's the least of it. A new church, now, there's a new land, an unexplored country."

"Will Green says there are savages in the New World," I offered, hoping to redirect the conversation. If we must talk, I would much rather it was about undiscovered lands than about religion. "They eat men's hearts."

Master Marlowe snorted. "Thou needst not cross the ocean to see men eating one another's flesh. The court at Greenwich will do for that." But he was not to be diverted from his musings for long. "And a new monarch, now, there's a new world as well," he went on. "Unknown and perilous. Wild beasts and volcanoes at every turn."

My hand jerked a little and nearly made a blot. Carefully I lifted the pen a few inches above the paper and made sure it would not drip before I spoke again. "A new monarch?"

"Thou'rt such an innocent, Richard. Aye, a new monarch. Didst think Gloriana, the most blessed, most regal queen of all England, would live forever?"

I was startled by this idea. Elizabeth had been on the throne of England since well before I was born. Of course, if I had thought of it, I would have known that she could not reign forever. But somehow I had not thought of it. She was the heretic daughter of a heretic king, and yet . . . England without Elizabeth?

"She is not so aged," I objected. "Surely there are many years yet."

"She has nine-and-fifty years. 'Tis only white powder hides her wrinkles now."

"But . . ." My pen was still suspended in the air above my paper. "But who will rule after her?"

Elizabeth, of course, was the Virgin Queen. She had no children.

"If there were any prophet who knew, his fortune would be made," Master Marlowe said dryly. "She's too sly for that. The minute she names an heir, every hanger-on at the court would be off to dance attendance on him, and who would care for an elderly queen tottering on her throne? She keeps them all in suspense, as she's ever done."

"But who might it be?" I was puzzling over it. The queen had no children, and neither her brother or sister, both of them dead now, had gotten an heir for England. Who did that leave?

Master Marlowe did not answer me at once. He finished trimming his nails and sat, staring into the fire, lightly and carefully stroking the ball of his thumb over the sharp little blade until I thought he had forgotten the question. But then he said suddenly, "James of Scotland."

"Who, sir?"

His sigh was a prayer for patience. "Hast not been listening? James VI, King of Scotland, her cousin a few times removed. Many think he'll be the next king. He's Protestant, and of the right age, and wise enough. Of course, there is the trifling difficulty that Elizabeth cut off his mother's head. 'Tis just possible he may bear England a grudge for that."

"Mary, Queen of Scots," I said slowly.

"Aye, of course. Scots," Master Marlowe pointed out, "live in Scotland."

I thought you were working for the Queen of Scots, Master Marlowe had said to his friend Pooley. I glanced up at him quickly, but he seemed to be thinking of something else.

"And there are others," he continued. "The Stanleys and the Seymours; they're English and her cousins as well. But they're also cousins to Jane Grey, and when she made a bid for the throne, she paid for it with her head. That might dissuade a man from making the attempt. And of course . . ."

"Sir?"

"There's the Infanta," Master Marlowe answered. "King Philip's daughter by his third wife. Or his second, I forget. The Spanish princess."

"But Spain is our enemy," I objected, baffled. Five years ago Philip of Spain had sent a fleet of ships to England's shores, bent on conquering England and returning it to the true faith.

I would rejoice to see England Catholic again, but I'd no wish to see it happen at the points of Spanish swords. I had cheered with the rest when I heard that God's winds and English courage had turned the Armada back. How could the daughter of our would-be conqueror lay a claim for the throne?

"Aye, Spain is our enemy now. But Philip has English blood as well as Spanish, and he is still Elizabeth's brother-in-law, do not forget. He was her sister's husband. That might bring him or his daughter closer than a cousin in Scotland. Particularly if the claim comes backed with enough Spanish troops."

I sat up straighter, as a shiver, both cold and warming, ran up my spine. "But she is . . ."

"She is Catholic. You begin to grasp it now. So . . . Scotland, England, or Spain? Protestant or papist?" He held out his hands, palm up, with the knife in one, and weighed them like a scale. "A man might become anything when the world changes."

"We might be Catholic again?" I had never thought it was possible. And yet, had it not happened once, before my birth, when Elizabeth's older sister, Mary, held the throne?

"Catholic, Protestant, Jew, Moslem," Master Marlowe said airily, "for all I know, or anyone else either." He got to his feet and tossed the penknife on the table. "I'm off. Have that done when I return."

Catholic again. I might be free one day to pray for my father's soul in church, as should be done. To light candles to my saints and say the old prayers without fear, without the constant worry that someone might be listening, spying, waiting to betray me.

And yet—a Spanish queen? A foreign monarch on the throne? I was a Catholic, but an English Catholic. To see England subject to her enemy . . .

My mind spun. Catholic and Spanish? English and Protestant? Why was there no third way? Why could I not pray in Latin and still remain an honest subject of my English queen?

It was too hard a problem for me. And in any case, why should I trouble my mind about it? The succession would be as it would be, without the least help from me. Someone would take the throne after Elizabeth, and all I could do was wait to see who.

And in the meantime, I had work to do. I settled myself back to my copying, but had not finished half a page before I was interrupted by Mistress Stavesly's voice from below.

"Richard! Come down, lad!" Carefully I wiped the pen clean, laid it aside, put the cork in the ink bottle, and ran downstairs to see what was needed.

I found Sam from the playhouse with Mistress Stavesly in her shop. Simple Moll, in a fit of shyness, was peeking at him from around a corner. I patted her on the shoulder as I went by. "'Tis only a 'prentice player, Moll. Yes, mistress?"

"Richard, knowst where thy master is?" Mistress Stavesly asked.

"No, truly," I answered.

"This lad says he's needed at the playhouse."

"Master Henslowe sent me," Sam confirmed. "He said to bring him at once, even if he was drinking or whoring."

Mistress Stavesly aimed a slap at him and he hopped back out of range, grinning impudently. "Mind thy manners, imp! Richard, go and fetch thy master."

"But I know not where he is," I protested.

She laughed. "Hast served him this long and knowst not where to look for him when he's lost? The taverns, i'faith. Now be off out of my shop, I've customers to mind."

So Sam went back to the playhouse, and I set out to search the taverns of London.

Master Marlowe was not in the Black Bull, or the Four Swans, or the Crown. But the tapster at the Mermaid advised me to try the Green Dragon, and there indeed he was, at a table in the far corner, sitting with his back to the door. The man he was speaking to was hunched over with his elbows on the table. A dark red velvet hat shadowed his face, a white plume on it swaying gently as he shook his head. The feather almost looked like a live thing, alert and suspicious, on watch for its master.

And the man's voice, when I heard it, made me shiver.

"Nay, Kit, prithee, listen. As thy friend, I tell thee, 'tis not wise."

Smooth, gentle, affectionate. Melting butter. Oil flowing over honey.

"I'll do it no more!" snapped Master Marlowe. His voice was low, but almost desperate. "You may tell them. With what I know, they cannot touch me."

"'Tis not a good time, Kit, to be forming new allegiances."

"Master Marlowe!" I said quickly, loudly. I had been warned, and more than once. They must neither of them turn and find me listening. By calling loudly for their attention, I would look all innocence.

Master Marlowe's head jerked up as if he'd been touched by a whip. The other man barely moved. Only his eyes shifted to me.

"You're wanted at the playhouse, master," I said, hoping that the faint quiver in my voice was only audible to my own ears. "Master Henslowe sent Sam to fetch you."

"Did Henslowe say what he wanted?" Master Marlowe asked.

"No, sir. Sam only said 'twas urgent."

"I must go, then," he said, and reaching into a pocket, he pulled out a few coins and scattered them across the table. "Farewell, Pooley," he added as he rose, without looking at his companion.

"Farewell, Kit," Pooley said, still gently.

Outside the tavern Master Marlowe turned to me. "Didst hear aught of what was said in there?" he asked, jerking his head toward the door.

Unbidden, my fingers went up to rub my left ear. "No, master, I heard nothing," I said earnestly.

He eyed me carefully and then nodded. "Good. Well done." He took his way toward the playhouse and left me wondering if what had been well done was my failure to hear, or my lying.

chapter twelve

NOVEMBER-
DECEMBER 1592

Master Marlowe delivered my clean copy of *The Massacre at Paris* to the Rose, and Master Henslowe divided up the parts among the players. Even Robin was given a role, although without a word to speak, as a lady-in-waiting to the Queen of France.

Henslowe had hoped to perform the *Massacre* in the fall. But before the players could learn their parts, the playhouse was forced to close for the winter. No one could act on that stage, open to the sky, in the midst of rain or snow. By the time Henslowe shut down at last, the players were already grumbling about chilblains and frozen toes.

There was still work to be done, however, even if the stage was empty. Master Henslowe shut himself up to read scripts, looking for new plays to perform in the spring. The players studied new parts. Robin and the apprentices went on learning, practicing speeches and tumbling and fencing as well as they could in the cramped lodgings of one player or another. And Will and his father spent the winter months going over the playhouse's costumes, checking every seam, scrubbing every stain, tightening every loose point or lace.

Nor was the playmaker idle. Master Marlowe was writing a new play, and this time in collaboration. The mild-eyed playmaker I had once seen at the Rose was working on it with him. Master Marlowe did not introduce him to me, of course, but Robin told me his name. It was William Shakespeare.

"But must they cut out her tongue?" he asked plaintively as they were at work one cold afternoon in Master Marlowe's lodgings.

"Of course they must," Master Marlowe answered impatiently. "She must be silenced, else she'll tell all she knows. And what, pray, would become of our plot then?"

"But to cut off her hands as well . . ."

"Or she will write down who ravished her." In the bedchamber, which I was trying to set to rights, I shivered, and ran the thumb of my left hand along the scar that marked my right palm. The wound had healed clean, but the scar was red, and raised, and stiffened my hand slightly, making it hard for me to stretch out my fingers completely.

I tried to shrug off the chill that had touched me and went back to straightening the bed. Master Marlowe slept as though he had nightmares. Each morning I found the blankets twisted and tangled into knots.

"Richard!"

I looked up through the open door. "Yes, master?"

"Take thyself off."

"I have not finished cleaning, sir."

"He makes less noise than a mouse in the wall," Master Shakespeare said, giving me a friendly smile.

"Aye, 'twill pull my nerves to pieces, listening to him make no noise," Master Marlowe grumbled. "Get thee gone, Richard, we've work to do here."

I was well used to being ordered from the room when Master Marlowe was writing, and I did not take it ill. Winter had the city in a tight grip by now, and it was too cold to wander the streets. But Mistress Stavesly never minded if I spent an hour or two in her kitchen.

When I came into the bakery, Mistress Stavesly was handing a few pence in change to a customer. He had an ordinary, friendly face, not one that would call attention. But I had seen that hat before, red velvet with the white plume quivering gently in a warm draft from the oven.

The man's eyes flicked to me for an instant as I came down the stairs, and then he nodded in farewell to

Mistress Stavesly and was gone.

"Mistress?" I asked. "Who was that man?"

Surely there were many red velvet hats in London. Surely I had no need to feel afraid.

"Nay, how should I know his name?" Mistress Stavesly went back to kneading dough, working it vigorously with her floury hands. "He liked my apple tart, that is all I know of him. A pleasant gentleman. Why, dost know him?"

"No." I had a strange urge to run upstairs and give a warning to Master Marlowe. To tell him—what? That a man with a red hat had bought an apple tart from Mistress Stavesly? And in any case, he had warned me not to pay heed to his affairs. Well, then, I would not.

But suddenly Mistress Stavesly's kitchen did not seem such a warm and welcoming place as usual. "I must go, I've an errand," I muttered, and risked Master Marlowe's ire by returning upstairs for my cloak. By the time I reached the street, the man in the red hat was nowhere to be seen.

And what would I do now? I might drink hot wine or sack in a tavern, but it was better to save up my small store of coins against the day I would leave Master Marlowe's service. Since I could not stay in the lodgings or the bakery, that left one place where I might keep dry and warm for free. Accordingly, I turned my steps toward the Rose.

The players might have decamped from the bare stage, but Master Henslowe would on no account suffer the costumes to be taken out of the playhouse. The silks and velvets and lace and leather were worth more, he said, than the building itself, and the thought of them being dropped in the street, or torn, or stolen by a rival playhouse was enough to make him look ill.

So Will cut and stitched and labored in the cramped tireroom, and when Master Marlowe had no use for my services, I sometimes joined him. He was always glad for company, and told me tales of strange lands and stranger people, farther from England, it seemed to me, than heaven is from earth.

I tried to keep quiet and listen—easily done, since Will liked well to talk. It was not that I had nothing to say in return. But I was afraid, if I let many words out, that something might show in my voice or my face, that he might look up from his needle and thread one day and read the truth in my eyes.

It would have been safer to avoid the playhouse altogether. But I was not wise or strong enough to do so.

This day I found Will, not in the tireroom, but just leaving the playhouse, wrapped in a dark blue cloak with the hood pulled up over his head. "Richard!" He hailed me with a wave. "I was choking in that room. My father's given me leave to walk for an hour and breathe the fresh air. Come down to the river with me."

So we walked to the bank of the Thames, where between the poor houses and crowded tenements we could catch glimpses of the river and the ships. The sunshine was thin and weak, the wind bitter, and I shivered despite my new cloak with the sheepskin collar, given to me by Master Marlowe. Will, however, drank the frigid air in deep gulps, a smile on his face.

"There are cannibals in the New World," he told me cheerfully. "I've just been reading of it."

"Cannibals!" I shuddered. "Why you want to go there, I cannot imagine."

Will laughed. "You have no heart for adventure, Richard." He pushed his hood back to look up at the pale winter sky, and I saw a bruise, still fresh and blue-purple, over his cheekbone.

"Will! What happened to your face?"

All Will's cheerfulness vanished in an instant. He scowled and walked quicker. "My father. He thought I needed a reminder yesterday to keep my mind on my work."

We walked in silence for a moment or two. Then I spoke, hoping to turn Will's mind back to more pleasant things.

"How do you know there are cannibals? Have people seen them at their feasts?"

Will gave me a rueful smile, as if to say he knew what I was trying to do, but he still answered. "A sailor with the Italian, Columbus, when they first landed, he went into a native's hut and found a man's thighbone cooking in a pot."

"Disgusting! But then . . ."

"But what?"

"How did he know it was a man's thighbone? Does it look so different from a pig's or a cow's? Could he tell at first glance?" Especially, I thought, if it was in a very thick stew or a pottage. Heaven only knew what kind of meat had been in some of the stews I had eaten.

"Marry, I know not," Will answered, smiling more naturally now. "I have not made examination myself. But so it says in the book. A man's thighbone. They kill and eat their aged and their sick."

"Then they eat only tough old meat, or pestilent," I pointed out. "It seems a shame."

I had hoped to make him laugh, and did so. Being with him made me think of the day my father had returned from one of his trips to London, bringing with him an unheard-of treat—two oranges, one for Robin and one for me. I remembered that astonishing burst of sweetness in my mouth, so vivid I was thirsty for more even as the first bite slid down my throat. It was like swallowing sunlight. That's what Will Green was to me.

And to him I was only shy little Richard Archer, an orphan and a stranger he was kind to. I knew that well enough. He was glad for my company, since he liked company, and would have been glad for anyone to talk to as he sat and sewed in the room that seemed such a prison to him. But the sight of me did not make his face light up the way the sight of a three-masted ship on the river did.

And if I had shown myself to him in a skirt and bodice, my hair miraculously restored, what would he have said to me? Nothing. He would not recognize his new friend Richard if he were to see Rosalind.

"Boys!" It was a soft, sweet voice with a little laugh in it. I looked up with a start. We were passing a small, shabby store, the plaster flaking off the walls, a red cardinal's hat on the sign. A woman stood in the doorway and stretched a hand out to us.

"You look like sweet, tender young boys. A shilling for the pair of you. Come in and warm yourselves, why not?"

Her smile was broad, her painted lips stretching wide. She should have been pretty. But her cheeks were too thin, her eyes desolate.

"Thank you, no, mistress," Will called back indifferently, not breaking his stride.

"Come back another time, my dears. . . ." Her voice faded away behind us.

"That was . . ." Words failed me. "Will, she was . . ."

"Aye, of course. Why, do you wish to go back?"

"No!" I could not help looking over my shoulder, even so.

"Have you lived in London all these months and never seen a whore?" Will asked, amused.

Perhaps I had and simply not known it. I had seen shops often enough with the cardinal's hat on the sign, but I had never known what it stood for.

"What a country innocent you are, Richard," Will teased me. "You'll die of the shock unless you accustom yourself to London ways."

I knew I must seem a fool to him, and yet I could not tell him why I felt compelled to look back at the woman a third time. She had called out to a man walking behind us, and now he stopped. She laid a hand on his arm and drew him closer.

If I had not fought off that apprentice my first day in London, if Master Marlowe had not taken me in. . . .

"'Tis only . . . she looked so sad," I said feebly to Will.

"Sad?"

"Aye. Did you not see?"

Will shrugged. "She looked like any other stale to me.

There!" He stopped and pointed to a tall ship. "See, that's the *Swallow*. She's back from Mexico. Can you imagine it, Richard, Mexico? They say 'tis like hottest summer all the year round, and the jungle is so thick a man must cut his way through it, and it springs up again behind him. Can you imagine?"

"I cannot," I said softly. My mind was still on the woman we had passed, and on the unhappiness that Will had not even seen. But I tried to speak more brightly, to tease Will in my turn and keep him from noticing my abstraction. "I cannot imagine any sight worth packing myself into such a listing, leaking rowboat as that—"

But Will paid no heed. "Listen, Richard." He turned to face me. "Tell no one, promise me?"

"I promise," I vowed, confused at his eager manner.

"The *Swallow* has need of a new crew. So I've heard the sailors say down at the docks. She will be some months revictualling and making repairs, but when she sails again in the spring—"

"Will, thou wouldst not!" I was so startled I did not notice that I'd dropped into the familiar "thou" with him for the first time. "What of thy father? He would never give thee leave."

"What of my father?" Will demanded angrily. "He has not bought me! I am not his by contract!"

"But thou owest him—obedience, dost not?" I faltered, seeing that I was saying everything he wanted least to hear. "Will, thou hast—a family, a trade. Thou hast a *place.*" It was what I had once had myself, what I could never have now that I spent each day as a living lie in my breeches and doublet. I had no place, no more than a ghost might, nowhere to be at home and at rest. "Wilt throw all of that away?"

"Aye!" Will boiled with fury. "'Sblood, Richard, you talk like my father. A place, as if that's all that matters! A worm has a place, too, but 'tis naught but a hole in the ground. Should I stay in my hole, then, just because 'tis mine?"

Yes. Yes, else thou'lt be lost all thy life, adrift with no anchor and no harbor. That was what I wished to say to him. But he had no notion of the value of what he was throwing so carelessly away, any more than Faustus in Master Marlowe's play had known the value of his soul when he gave it over to the devil. I knew Will would not hear me.

I hated the awkward silence between us, but knew not how to break it. At last Will spoke.

"You'll not tell?"

"Of course not. I never would." I could not keep the touch of reproach from my voice. "I would not break my word."

"Aye, I know." But he was not pleased with me, and I could have bitten my tongue off for questioning him, for quarreling with him. He had been so happy with his plan, and I had only told him what was wrong with it.

"I—I must go," I said awkwardly. "My master may need me." This was a lie. Master Marlowe wouldn't want me back for another hour at least.

I hated leaving him without a warmer word, and I lingered, until at last Will looked up and gave me a brief smile. It was not the wide grin I loved to see, but at least it showed he was not angry with me.

"Farewell, Richard."

It was the kindest leave-taking I could hope for, and I was glad to have it. But it was poor, thin food indeed to feed my hungry heart.

chapter thirteen
december 1592-
january 1593

Master Marlowe, it seemed, did not keep Christmas. "I've no money to waste pouring sack down other men's throats," he snapped when I innocently asked if there would be any guests during the Twelve Nights.

The meanest home in the city had a sprig of yew or holly over the door, but Master Marlowe's chambers remained as bare as ever, and on Christmas Eve he sat in his rooms writing while Moll and Mistress Stavesly and I feasted downstairs on veal pie and custard.

On Twelfth Night I did not expect anything different. Master Marlowe had been hard at work all afternoon and looked as if he planned to keep writing half the night. But as the evening darkened and I began to think of lighting the candles, he surprised me by throwing down his pen and rising suddenly enough to shove the stool across the floor and tip it over.

"There, Richard, thou mayst copy that tonight," he said. "'Tis the new first scene. Master Shakespeare will want to read it. Well, what?"

"Nothing, sir," I said glumly, seeing my plans for the evening fall into ruins.

"Oh? Thou lookst like thou hast lost thy dearest love." He'd gone into his bedchamber by then and spoke to me through the half-open door. "What is't?"

"Master Cowley, sir . . ." I let the sentence die away, unsure how to word it so that it would not sound like a reproach.

"And what about Master Cowley—oh." The words were muffled, as if he were pulling a shirt over his head, and then he appeared in the doorway, fastening up the buttons on his velvet doublet. "He invited thee as well, did he?"

"My brother asked him for me, sir." Master Cowley had opened his home to all the players on this, the last day of Christmas. "I thought you would go yourself," I added.

"Oh, I will. Well, do not look so downcast, Richard. Thou mayst go. Leave the copying for tomorrow." When I looked up with eager thanks, he waved me off. "And tell him I will be there later. I've an errand first."

He finished dressing and left, hatless but with a warm cloak wrapped around him, as I retrieved the fallen stool, stoppered the ink bottle, and stacked the scattered pages. I blew on the top sheet to dry it and I glanced down at the words my master had written, curious to see what I would be copying tomorrow.

What sort of name was this for a character? Saturnius. Latin? I must ask Robin. And what words had Master Marlowe given him to speak? "Noble patricians, patrons of my right, defend the justice of my cause with arms," he proclaimed.

Saturnius, it seemed, thought that he should be the next emperor. But a little way down the page, another character had different ideas. "Romans, fight for freedom in your choice," he urged.

I stood still, holding the page in my hand. What did Master Marlowe and Master Shakespeare think they were about? To open a play with two claimants for a throne, when no one knew who would be the next to wear the crown of England? Did they think that because the play was set in ancient times no one would notice?

Of course, Master Marlowe must know better than I did how to write a play. But I was beginning to think that I knew better than he did how to hide. Why should a man with as many secrets as my master be eager to draw attention to himself with such a play as this?

Shaking my head, I put the page back down. In some

ways Master Marlowe was a kind master, if I put from my mind what had happened the night I'd overheard him talking to Pooley. He did not ask much work of me; he never grudged me as much as I could eat; he'd given me leave to go out to the night's festivities. But nevertheless, eight more months of his service was beginning to seem an eternity.

With a sigh, I wrapped myself in my cloak and headed out into the night. The air was bitter, and the cobblestones were slick with a light frost. But at least the cold cut the smells of summer to something more bearable. Candlelight glowed yellow behind windows; snatches of song and laughter drifted from dwellings and taverns and ordinaries as I walked through the streets.

Master Cowley's house, when I reached it, was full of light and noise. No one answered my knock—likely no one had heard it—so I edged around the open door and slipped inside.

The fire had been piled high and there were candles burning. Food was spread out on the board—a good piece of cold pork, pies, cheese, gingerbread. My mouth watered. Players sat at the table, stood by the hearth; the colors of their best clothes glowed in the firelight like stained glass. Nick had grabbed hold of Harry and was attempting to use him to demonstrate the steps of a

French almain, but it threatened to turn into a wrestling match rather than a dance. Master Alleyn and Master Henslowe sat on a bench betting at primero, Master Alleyn dealing the cards.

Six months ago I would have been shocked to find myself in such company. But now I could not help laughing as Sander, outraged at some insult, chased Sam about the room until Master Cowley seized hold of them, one collar in each hand.

"Goodwill toward men!" he bellowed. "And peace in this house, if not on this earth!" He released them both with a shove toward the laden table. "Eat, drink, and be merry, I command you!"

They were only boys, I thought tolerantly, smiling. Even the grown men seemed tonight as lighthearted as Robin and the other apprentices. They might act adultery and murder and wickedness on the stage, but they were ordinary enough when their feet were on the ground.

None of them had noticed me.

Usually I was content to have it so. They all thought of Richard Archer as timid, and it was for the best that they should. They did not expect me to say much. Indeed, in the company of players, it was difficult to draw attention even if you wished it, and easy enough to stay unnoticed in the background.

But that did not mean it did not, at times, get lonely there.

Before I had a moment to sink into self-pity, however, Robin dashed up to me, his cheeks bulging with a mouthful of gingerbread. "Thou'rt here!" he cried, scattering crumbs. "Look, there's food enough for all!" He pulled me into the thick of the crowd.

I gave Robin his new year's gift, a small bag I'd sewn from scraps of wool and filled with nuts and a few apples from the fall, a little soft now but still sweet. He had a present for me as well, an orange the size of a walnut, made out of sweet marchpane. We ate savory brawn with sharp mustard, and cheese, and sweet cakes with nutmeg and ginger. Robin got us tankards of lambswool, steaming hot cider with a white froth on top, and we joined the other apprentices playing snapdragon at one end of the table.

And what did it matter, after all, I thought, as Nat sprinkled raisins into a pewter bowl full of burnt wine and Sander touched a candle to the liquid so that it burst into blue flame. Was it such a weighty thing that they did not know the truth of me, that Rosalind would not have been welcome here as Richard was? When I had yet been almost a stranger to these boys, they had run to my defense. Surely that goodwill was true, and deeper than any disguise I might wear. Surely that went to the heart.

Sam, as impetuous as ever, tried to snatch a raisin out of the fire but yelped and jumped away to suck his burnt fingers. Laughter filled up the room, and the players came near to watch. Sander tried, and Robin, and Nat. All failed.

I met Robin's eyes over the table, and he smiled, but his eyes glistened with unshed tears. We had played this at our last Twelfth Night. Robin's friend Hal had been the first to save a raisin from the flames. Our father had been there, watching, laughing. What a strange mixture grief and joy made, blended together inside me.

"Take thy turn, Richard," Sander urged.

"A penny on Richard to do it," a voice said behind me. I glanced around to see Will. We had not spoken since that day by the river, when we had almost quarreled.

"He has clever fingers," Will said, nodding to me in encouragement. "Do not fail me, Richard, I've no pennies to spare."

The blue flames, eerie and beautiful, danced over the surface of the liquid, the raisins floating under them, plump dark spots in the brightness. It was a matter of patience, I thought, not courage. No good to snatch at the first moment that offered. You must watch for a gap in the flames, seize your chance—

I darted my fingers in, pinched up a raisin, and got it

safely away. The players clapped and cheered and Will slapped me on the back.

"Well done, Richard!" He grabbed his winnings off the table. "Come, a moment, I've something for you."

Surprised, I followed him to a quiet corner near the door. "A good new year to you," Will said, digging a hand in his purse and pulling out a small package swathed in linen and tied with a red cord.

"A— a gift?" I stammered, awkward. "No need—"

"And when has a gift been for need? Open it, pray. Or I'll think you do not want it and be mortally offended."

I laughed a little shakily and loosened the cord. Out of the linen wrappings, a small wooden pipe fell into my hand.

"Oh," I said weakly. That day we had sat side by side on the bench outside the tobacconist's shop. That day Will had been so brave.

"You need one of your own," Will said easily. "Why, Richard, what is't?"

"I thought—you might be angry with me," I muttered, not daring to look up at him. My voice trembled ridiculously.

"Angry? For speaking your mind to me? Richard, truly, you worry far too much. When you never said a word of reproach to me for getting you into a brawl that day and—what's this?"

I must take some action quickly, or I'd likely betray myself. "Here," I said hurriedly, stuffing a roll of linen into his hand. "A good new year."

He unrolled the cloth, looking with surprise at my offering. It was a collar of fine lawn. Master Green had let me have the scraps from a few shirts. There had not been enough to make a ruff, but I'd been able to piece together a collar and embroider it around the edges with leaves and vines in white thread, coiling and curling and unfolding. I'd not been sure I'd have a chance to give it to him, but I'd tucked it inside my doublet just in case.

"There's hours of work in this. Richard, I'm almost shamed."

"We are friends, then?"

"When did we stop?"

It was risky, but I glanced at his face. His smile was friendly, his blue eyes baffled a little. He was taller than I was; the top of my head came only to his chin. If I lifted up on my toes, my lips would just meet his. I blushed at the thought.

Then Master Marlowe saved me. The door beside us thumped open, and he stood leaning with one hand against the doorframe. His cloak was gone, his hair disheveled, and one side of his face, from jaw to cheekbone, was scraped raw. A trickle of blood from his nose had smeared his chin and spotted his crisp white ruff.

"Well, do not stand and stare," he said impatiently when he noticed me. "Find some water, so I do not drip blood on the food."

Thieves, he said, as the players crowded around in alarm. He'd been set on in an alley but had fought them off, and he was entirely fine, and had we nothing better to do than fuss and bother him? By that time I was back from the kitchen with a bowl of water, and Master Marlowe pulled a handkerchief from his sleeve, soaked it, and found himself a seat by the fire to clean his wounds.

"Are you truly well, master?" I asked him anxiously. He had wiped his bloody nose and was dabbing gingerly at the long scrape on his face. The flesh about the eye on that side was also tender and starting to swell.

"Aye, aye, leave be." He reached out to dip the handkerchief in the bowl of water that I still held, and paused for a moment, looking at his hand as if it belonged to someone else. I looked down as well, and saw that his palm and fingers were coated and sticky with half-dried blood.

I gasped in alarm, thinking he was more seriously hurt than he knew, and was about to call Master Cowley for aid when he shook his head to silence me.

"'Tis not mine," he said, his voice low. He scrubbed fiercely at his hand and then threw the blood-stained handkerchief at me as if it disgusted him to touch it. "Take that and begone. And bring me some sack." He did not meet my eyes.

I made my way back to the kitchen to dispose of the dirty water and the soiled handkerchief. No washing would get so much blood out of white linen. It was only fit for a rag now.

"Thieves," Master Alleyn was saying as I passed him, shaking his head. "The city is scarcely safe to walk in these days."

"And on Twelfth Night of all nights," Master Cowley added. "They have no shame."

It was strange, I thought, that thieves would try to rob a gentleman with a sword. It might happen, of course. Men could be desperate. But surely thieves most often tried for easier prey. And indeed, if the blood on Master Marlowe's hand told a story, at least one of the men who had attacked him had paid dearly for his boldness.

I brought my master his sweet wine. He gave me no thanks, but only took a deep swallow.

Master Alleyn was singing now, and Sander plucked a lute to accompany him. "'Tomorrow the fox will come to town,'" he sang. He must be cheerful indeed to indulge in such an old country song, nothing new or fashionable about it. Will was part of the group who joined cheerfully in the chorus, "'Oh, keep you all well there!'" But I did not go over to them. Best to remain here, quietly, and stay out of notice, and let Will forget how absurdly I had behaved over a simple gift. Master Marlowe might not approve if I shared the bench with him, so I sat down on the hearth near his feet.

"'I must desire you, neighbors all, to hallow the fox out of the hall,'" sang Master Alleyn. The small room was full of warmth and merriment and light, and my master and I sat silent to one side, watching together.

chapter fourteen
february 1593

The snow had barely melted from the streets when Master Henslowe opened the playhouse again. And the first play upon the stage was to be, of course, *The Massacre at Paris*.

Despite the chill remaining in the air, Master Marlowe indulged in his strange preference for washing. To my relief, once I had brought the water, he sent me out to fetch his linen from the laundry. I dawdled as long over the errand as I could, and when I returned, I found him fastening up the gilt buttons on his velvet doublet. He did not seem to have noticed my lateness. "Thou'lt come with me," was all he said.

I might have objected, or told him I felt ill and begged him to excuse me. But in his eye there was that faint look of mockery and challenge that I had seen before, the reminder that he knew about the rosary hidden under my shirt and doublet. So I did not protest or even ask his reason.

Though we arrived early, the Rose was nearly full, and there was a long line before the door. "I hear 'tis bloody, very bloody," I heard a woman say eagerly as we made our way past.

"Aye, and 'tis true, every word," her companion answered.

As we entered, Master Marlowe was spied by Master Henslowe, who came to greet him, calling out his name. Soon he was surrounded by a knot of friends, congratulating him and wishing him well.

Master Marlowe had been silent all the way from his lodgings—not a silence of ease, but one of tension and nerves. Now, suddenly, he broke into a quick patter of words and jests and laughter.

"William!" He seized his fellow playmaker by the hand. "And soon 'twill be our play on the stage. How dost thou?"

"Well, I thank you." Master Shakespeare smiled gently. His calm manner only seemed to heighten Master Marlowe's restless energy. "Good fortune, Kit."

But Master Marlowe's attention had already turned to someone else, a tall, sour-faced man in sober brown who tried to edge past unnoticed. Master Marlowe shot out a hand to catch him by the sleeve.

"Thomas! It gives me joy to see thee," Master Marlowe

exclaimed, beaming as if the newcomer were his long-lost brother. "'Tis kind, 'tis very kind of thee to come. And art thou well?"

The man tugged his arm free from the playmaker's grasp. "I am well, I thank you," he answered coldly. "'Tis your own welfare you should be concerned with, Marlowe, and not that of your body. Take thought for your soul."

Master Marlowe did not seem in the least offended by the man's condemnation or his cold use of "you" to answer such a kind greeting. He grinned affectionately. "Still so concerned for me, art thou, Thomas? Thou wast not so worried a year past, when we shared a room together. A few coins to clink in thy purse and thou canst afford to cast off old friends, is't not so?"

His back stiff and his face pinched with disapproval, the stranger made a formal little bow to the company and moved off. "But I take it kindly thou hast risked thy soul and come to see my play!" Master Marlowe called after him, laughing to see his shoulders flinch a little as people turned to see who called out so loudly.

Master Henslowe shook his head. "I've not seen Thomas Kyd here for close to a year," he said, surprised. "Once he came to every play, but now . . ."

"Oh, he had a touch of ague and thought it was the

plague," Master Marlowe answered dismissively. "Since then he's turned half Puritan. I cannot think the Almighty enjoys an aspect of perpetual gloom, any more than his neighbors do, but—" He fell silent, his chin lifting as he looked across to the entrance of the playhouse. And the silence seemed to spread out from him, like ripples from a stone dropped into still water.

The man who had just come through the door was in the midst of a crowd, and yet it was easy to see that he was the one they all followed. It was not just the way they hesitated, waiting for his motion to determine where they should go. It was something, too, in the way he stood, a sense of ease, as though he knew and had always known that he had only to ask and have.

His dark beard came to a neat point, and there were pearls hanging from both his ears. I had thought Master Marlowe's velvet doublet magnificent, but the cost of this man's clothing might have beggared a small village. His white satin doublet shone as if polished, and the black damask cloak thrown carelessly over his shoulder was stiff with gold embroidery.

Slowly whispers crept into the silence, like bubbles rising in a pot on the fire until it seethed and roiled with heat.

"'Tis not—"

"Aye, it must be—"

"*Raleigh!*"

"The queen locked him in the Tower."

"Aye, but 'twas only for marrying. She has a jealous heart. He'll be her favorite again, mark my words."

"Nay, a traitor—"

"An *atheist*—"

"Hush thy foolish tongue!"

The man scanned the crowd lazily, smoothed the chalk-white gloves on his hands, and walked over to where Master Marlowe stood. His followers swirled after him like the tail to a horse, and the common folk pressed back to leave them space. Master Marlowe bowed, sweeping his hat off his head, and said smoothly, "Sir Walter, I am honored beyond expression. I had no thought of seeing you here."

"Parliament meets, and so I've come to London," Sir Walter answered. "The country cannot content me all the year long." Delicately he held a small sphere up to his nose, the ivory carved into lacework so that the scents of spices and rosewater could sweeten the air he breathed.

Master Henslowe took this as a hint. "May I show your honor to the Lords' Rooms?" he asked, making a courtly bow of his own and gesturing toward the small chambers over the stage.

"I thank you," Sir Walter answered courteously. "I've heard that this play is your best, Kit. Do not disappoint me, I pray you."

Master Marlowe, frowning a little, seemed to be looking at something over Sir Walter's shoulder, but the mention of his name snapped his attention back where it belonged. "I'll stab myself to the heart for every moment of tedium I cost you," he promised extravagantly.

Sir Walter raised one eyebrow. "Well, that would enliven the performance, no doubt. Or perhaps the reverse, since adding one more corpse would only make the scene more deathlike. Aye, lead on, lead on," he said to Henslowe, and Master Marlowe went with them to see the knight to his seat. The air that they passed through seemed to sparkle a little behind them.

"What a crowd!" said a voice in my ear, and I turned to see Will beside me. "*Raleigh,* can you believe it? Thank heaven you're here, Richard. Come backstage, will you? We need another pair of hands. Another dozen would do us well, in truth—"

"Will, who is that over there, by the doors?"

He cast a hurried glance at the man I pointed out, the one who had captured Master Marlowe's attention even as he stood talking with a knight of the realm. He was short and slightly made, and seemed in no way extraordinary;

no one else paid the least heed to him. His clothing, like Sir Walter's, was black and white, but his doublet was dull black broadcloth, his shirt and ruff of plain linen. The only thing about him that might draw anyone's eye was that he carried one shoulder hunched a little higher than the other.

"It cannot be," Will murmured, his voice low and astonished. *"Robert Cecil?"*

"Who's he?"

"The queen's right hand, that's who he is," Will said, shaking his head. "Robert the devil, they call him." The thin figure, a little awkward with the hunch of his back, made its way into the middle galleries. Apparently, unlike Sir Walter, Robert Cecil did not care for the publicity and display of the Lords' Rooms over the stage.

"Why do they call him the devil?" I asked.

Will shrugged. "He's not one to cross, I suppose. Come, Richard, Sam's torn his petticoat, and Master Alleyn says his doublet is too short. Have mercy and help us, please?"

I hesitated, casting a glance after my master. Should I ask his permission before I vanished backstage? But he was keeping grand company; he would not wish to be troubled with me. And after all, he had only told me to accompany him to the playhouse. He had not told me I must stay in the yard and watch.

I'd thought the front of the playhouse crowded, but it was nothing to the confusion behind the scenes. Soon I had patched Sam's petticoat and tied Nat's ruff and tightened a button on Master Cowley's sleeve. Will knelt at Master Alleyn's feet, straightening the garters on his hose, while Master Green did his best to convince the aggrieved player that his black silk doublet was the perfect length.

"Do not move; that hem is coming loose," I said to someone standing before me in a pale green satin gown trimmed with narrow bands of black velvet. I did not even ascertain who wore it, but dropped to my knees to catch up the errant stitches before they unraveled further.

"That will do," I said as I bit off the thread and looked up to see to whom I had been ministering. My eyes traveled past the green skirts, the stomacher embroidered with yellow vines, the wide lace ruff, and up to the face, pale with white powder under a black wig.

"Robin?" I said in surprise, and got to my feet. "I hardly knew thee."

My little brother looked half sick with nerves. He opened his mouth to speak, but just then Master Alleyn's voice rose over all. "Oh, very well, very well, 'twill do. 'Tis time, masters, prepare yourselves!"

One of the points that fastened Robin's sleeve to his

bodice had come loose. I quickly retied it. "Thou'lt do well," I promised him. Master Cowley stood taller, straightened the crown on his head, and opened the door at the back of the stage to stride out into the view of the audience. The other players entered after him in a swirl of silks and velvets and rustling taffeta. Robin was swept up among them. Will flopped down on a table next to me with a sigh of relief.

"I thought we'd never get them ready," he whispered, only to receive a glare from Master Alleyn, who, as the Catholic villain Guise, was still waiting for his entrance. Will made an unrepentant face at the player's back, but hushed until he stalked onto the stage. There was an angry howl from the crowd to greet him, and under cover of the noise Will whispered to me again.

"Listen to them! I've never heard the groundlings shout so. Well, they may enjoy it, but 'tis not a play I care for."

I turned to him with sudden, unreasonable joy. "You do not?"

He gave me a sidelong glance, as if puzzled by my eagerness. "What tireman would? Pig's blood is a misery to get out of a costume."

I nodded, and tried to look sympathetic, and not as if, like a fool, I had expected him to say something completely different. Why should he dislike the play for any reason other than the extra work it made for him? Why should I expect him to hate it for the same reasons I did?

Will and I sat together backstage for the rest of the play. We could not see much of what was happening onstage, only occasional glimpses as the players came on and off. But we could hear. As the wicked Catholics pursued the innocent Protestants across the stage, they shouted lines I knew all too well.

"'There are a hundred Protestants which we have chased into the river Seine that swim about and so preserve their lives,'" Nick warned. "'How may we do? I fear me they will live.'"

"'Go place some men upon the bridge with bows and darts to shoot at them they see, and sink them in the river as they swim,'" answered Harry, bold with the glory of his first man's part.

"'Stab him and send him to his friends in hell,'" Master Alleyn roared.

And every time a player fell to the stage, miming death and smeared with blood, the crowd howled with rage. "Filthy papists!" "Rome is the devil!" I thought that Master Alleyn must fear for his life. When he was murdered in his turn, the watchers whooped and clapped so loudly that the play had to halt and the murderers hang uselessly about the stage with nothing to do until the noise died down enough to let them continue.

At last it was over. The players thronged backstage, laughing and talking. I looked, but did not see Robin among them. Will and his father hurried off to examine the damage to the costumes. And I slipped out into the yard to look for my master.

I found him sitting in the first gallery. Master Henslowe leaned on the railing, talking excitedly. "A triumph, Kit, 'twill keep the house full for a month, I warrant you," he was saying as I came up. But Master Marlowe answered only with an abstracted smile.

Master Henslowe hurried backstage to congratulate his players. The galleries emptied, and the last of the audience made its way out the doors. And still Master Marlowe sat, and I stood mutely by, waiting for him to tell me what he wished me to do.

Some of the hirelings came out and began to scrub the stage, pouring buckets of water over the sticky blood that the players had tracked all over the worn boards.

"'Tis only pig's blood," Master Marlowe said suddenly, and glanced aside at me. I do not know what he saw in my face, but he smiled, it seemed to me a little ruefully, and turned his eyes back to the stage. "Pig's blood and false speeches, and the groundlings are happy and will pay a penny apiece to see it. Henslowe's seats are filled, and the players are paid, and the playmaker has a brand-new reputation as a loyal Protestant. And who is harmed by it? 'Tis all dissembling, Richard." Now he looked directly at me. "'Tis a skill thou wouldst do well to practice." And before I could react he had risen, clasping his hands together overhead and stretching until his bones cracked. "Get thee home, then. I'll be out for some time."

Some of the audience were still gathered outside the Rose's door, talking over the play. I kept close to the wall of the playhouse, working my way past the crowd, and almost bumped into a figure my own height in pale green satin.

"Pardon, mistress," I murmured, without thinking, before my eyes took in the face, pale with powder, and the cropped hair. Robin's wig was gone, and he looked clownish and tragic at once, with red paint still brightening his mouth and his eyes rimmed in black. "*Robin?* What dost here?"

"I only wanted a breath of air," Robin muttered, his voice husky and odd.

"Master Henslowe will have thy head for stepping foot out of the playhouse in that gown," I warned him. "If Master Green does not take it first."

He nodded, as if he hardly cared.

"Robin? Art ill?"

"Thou wast right."

"About what?"

He shook his head in amazement. "About the play-house. Didst hear them?" He dropped his voice to a whisper. "Yelling for Catholic blood?"

I should have been triumphant. But how could I, seeing the white misery on his face under the gaudy paint?

"'Twas—'twas but one play, Robin," I said awkwardly, keeping my voice low as well so that those around us would not hear.

"'Twas my first time on the stage. They all expect me to be glad for it."

"Thou didst not write the speeches."

"I played my part."

"I wrote the play out myself," I countered. "Every word. I am at least as much to blame as thee. Thou didst not even have a line to speak."

"I was onstage." Robin looked ready to melt with guilt. "Thou wast right. I should never have stayed here."

I sighed and said to my little brother for the first time in our lives, "No, thou wast right."

He blinked.

"Thou hadst no other choice, Robin. Nor I. Where else could we have gone?"

The two of us could have begged for crusts of bread

like the old veteran and his little son by St. Paul's church-yard. Or I could have become like that woman under the sign of the cardinal's hat, selling myself to keep off hunger. I knew London better than I had six months ago. There were worse things than being a player or a play-maker's servant, and I had seen them.

We were safe, Robin and I. We had bread and clothes and beds at night. We were only doing what we must to keep ourselves alive.

God keep thee safe, Rosalind, my father had said. Perhaps, strange though it might be, the playhouse and the playmaker were God's way of answering the prayer.

"'Tis not truth, Robin," I told him. "'Tis pig's blood and false speeches. And who is . . ." I had meant to finish Master Marlowe's sentence. *And who is harmed by it?* But as I thought of the groundlings shrieking their blood-thirst, I could not say it. Instead, I reached out to grasp Robin's arm, feeling the solid flesh and bone beneath the slippery satin.

"We must survive," I whispered to him, my voice low and fierce. "We must go to their churches, take part in their plays, and keep the truth in our hearts."

Robin nodded and put his hand into mine, clasping it as if we had made a bargain.

"Get thee within," I said, with a faint attempt at a smile.

"And let no one see thee, or thou'lt have a beating for risking that gown."

Once Robin had gone, I made my way toward the bridge, passing groups of people walking slowly and talking. None noticed me as I slipped by. Just another servant boy, all but invisible in the slowly gathering dusk.

"Murdering papists."

"They'd kill us if they could."

"Spying for Spain, all of them, no doubt."

"And the Pope has ordered it. He said it would be no sin to kill our queen."

"Anyone might be a secret Catholic. Any neighbor, any servant, any friend . . ."

"God defend us!"

I felt cold reach all the way down my spine, a chill settle into my stomach. Hugging my arms across my chest, I hurried through the streets.

'Tis all dissembling . . . Pig's blood and false speeches . . . And who is harmed by it?

Meaning only to comfort Robin, I'd found Master Marlowe's words in my own mouth. And they had seemed true enough. No player had been injured on that stage, not so much as bruised. They would perform again tomorrow, none the worse for having their throats slit today.

Robin and I must survive. Surely it was no sin. Surely no one could blame us for only trying to live.

But as the sun faded behind clouds, and the early dark of a winter evening gathered, I thought of the groundlings, shrieking for the deaths of Catholics, and remembered my old neighbors, tearing my home apart. And one of them, it must have been, had whispered a word in the sheriff's ear. Who? Hugh Forrester, the father of Robin's friend Hal? Our maidservant, Joan? Master Crabbe at the school? Someone had seen my father cross himself, had glimpsed a lighted candle through our windows, had caught a whisper of a Latin prayer, and that had been enough.

They'd kill us if they could. . . . Anyone might be a secret Catholic. Any neighbor, any servant, any friend . . .

There were no neighbors or friends with such suspicion abroad. *We are all harmed by it,* I answered Master Marlowe in my mind.

may 1593

Spring came at last, and warmth with it. A haze of green softened the fields outside the city, and the hawthorn hedges bloomed white with their own snow of blossoms. It was on such a sweet, sunlit day that I went on my regular errand to pick up Master Marlowe's linen from the laundry.

Mistress Pieters's small shop was full, and everyone seemed to be talking, not waiting to be served. I squeezed my way inside and listened to scraps of conversation until I could catch Mistress Pieters's eye.

"... Spanish hunting us at home and the English here ..."

"... warned them, but no one cared to listen ..."

"Stay home tonight, who knows what might befall?"

"Richard?"

Mistress Pieters looked astonished and not well pleased to see me.

"I've come for Master Marlowe's collar and cuffs, please, mistress," I said, uneasy. I rather wished I could retreat out of the shop and come back another time, but it was impossible. The chatter had ceased and all eyes turned to me, and they were not friendly eyes, either.

"Indeed?" Mistress Pieters said at last, and her fair cheeks flushed red. "Master *Marlowe's* collar and cuffs?" She all but spat his name and, rummaging in a basket, snatched up the fine linen and threw it at me. "He has a nerve, to send you here today for these!"

I stared at her, bewildered, and held out the coins in my hand. "Mistress? What is it? I do not—"

"Thinkst thou we have not been by the church and seen what thy master has done there?" she snapped. "Take his property and begone! And I'll have none of his money, either. Tell him not to send thee to this shop again!"

Baffled, I left, feeling unfriendly gazes and angry thoughts prickling along the length of my spine. I had to fight the urge to break into a run as soon as I reached the street.

What on earth had Master Marlowe done? Mistress Pieters had said something about a church. But Master Marlowe had not set foot in a church since I'd been in his service.

That is, he had not set foot inside a *Protestant* church.

They were all Protestants, these Dutch. My stomach began to tighten and I walked quicker.

I had wondered if Master Marlowe might be a Catholic himself. Surely not. Not the man who'd forced me to swear on my saints to save my life. Not the man who had written that play, who had painted Catholics as bloody murderers for every Protestant in London to hate. Unless . . .*'Tis all dissembling, Richard,* he had said to me. How deep did his dissembling go? And what was the truth he was trying so hard to hide?

Something struck me in the middle of my back, something soft and slimy. I spun around in surprise, and the next missile hit over my heart. I gagged at the smell of ripe horse dung.

Who had thrown it? I looked around wildly. The woman walking by in her neat white coif, who snatched at her two children's hands to hurry them along? The wealthy man in the loose green gown and the tall black hat?

I was ready to run, when something stung the backs of my legs. Now I seemed under attack from two directions at once. Which way did safety lie, and which way danger?

"Playmaker's boy!"

It was a mocking hiss, with malice behind it. I whirled around again, and a pebble hit my cheek. I jumped back, covering my eye, and was about to flee—any direction must be better than standing still, a cowering target—when I heard a loud, angry voice.

"Wilt cause trouble in the streets, today of all days?" The speaker was a tall Dutchman. He had hauled a boy of Robin's age out of a dark alley, and now he wrenched a stone out of his upraised hand. The boy protested in quick Dutch, pointing at me, but the man snapped back at him in English. "Get thee home!" he ordered. His eyes met mine over the boy's head, and I knew the order was in truth meant for me.

The last time I had seen this man, it had been in the streets near the Rose, with mud and blood dripping from his fair hair.

I took his advice and ran.

In Broad Street, by the Dutch church, I was forced by a crowd to slow my steps. People clustered about the doorway of the church, but they seemed to be neither going in nor coming out. In my present mood, a crowd in front of a Protestant church was nothing I cared to encounter. But still I hesitated.

Thinkst thou we have not been by the church and seen what thy master has done there? Mistress Pieters's words seemed to imply that Master Marlowe had made some mark or left some sign that could still be seen. And now that I looked more closely, I realized that the crowd was thickest around a paper pasted up by the church door. A libel. Someone had written a message and posted it on the wall of the Dutch church for all of London to read. Presumably, from what Mistress Pieters had said, that someone had been Master Marlowe.

It was dangerous to stay. I might be recognized as Master Marlowe's servant at any moment. And had I not been warned, more than once, to pay no heed to my master's affairs?

But what if this libel revealed something of the elusive truth under Master Marlowe's dissembling?

"Richard! Thank God. Come back out of this mob."

I nearly shrieked aloud as a hand fell on my arm, and wrenched free to turn around and look up at Master Marlowe's face.

"Peace!" he snapped, pulling me a few steps away into an alley. "Dost want all London to hear thee?" His face twisted with disgust as he took in the state of my doublet. "Didst fall in the street? No matter. Go thou and read what it says, then come back and tell me." He was frowning anxiously, his lips thin, his face drawn.

"Read it?" I choked out, bewildered. Had not Master Marlowe written the libel himself? Why did he need me to tell him what it said?

"Of course, read it!" He gave me a shove back toward

the church. "I dare not go myself, too many know my face. But none will notice thee. Hurry!"

Now I understood nothing at all. Had he written the libel or not? I slipped out of the alley and made my way toward the church. Everyone was trying to do the same— get close enough to read the paper or listen to someone else read it aloud. Soon I was packed in, bodies on all sides of me, and I could see nothing over the broad shoulders of the man in front of me.

"What does it say?" I asked a man beside me.

"How can I see?" he answered impatiently. "Here, move on, if you've read it once!"

"Something about those immigrants," said a woman's spiteful voice from behind me, and a sharp elbow nudged me in the ribs.

"Who asked them to come here?"

"Not enough jobs for true Englishmen, and bread costs so much. . . ."

Well, I might not be able to see over men's shoulders, but there were some benefits after all to being short and thin. Using my shoulder as a wedge, I wormed my way in between the two men in front of me. There were grumbles and cries of "Wait thy turn," but I ignored them, pushing farther into the crowd. I even thought of dropping to my hands and knees and crawling between legs, but didn't try it for fear of being trampled. At last I wound up with my nose nearly pressed against the libel pasted to the church wall.

I had to push myself back a little to gain space in which to read. When I did, I saw that there was nothing unfamiliar about what the libel said. It was not, thank every saint, about Catholics. It only declared what those behind me in the crowd were saying, what I had heard a mob of apprentices shout at a Dutch stranger in the streets—that foreigners were vultures, devouring honest English workers like a glutton eats his dinner. Only the libel said it in rhyme. And the last few lines made me realize why Mistress Pieters had thrown me out of her shop, why she had refused to touch Master Marlowe's money.

> *Since words nor threats nor any other thing*
> *Can make you to avoid this certain ill,*
> *We'll cut your throats, in your temples praying,*
> *Not Paris Massacre so much blood did spill.*

Paris Massacre—that was nearly the name of Master Marlowe's new play. And across the bottom of the libel was a bold, black signature:

Tamburlaine

Master Alleyn, on the stage, a bloodthirsty tyrant in his

red doublet with the fur trim. Another play by Master Marlowe.

It was easier making my way out of the crowd than it had been to push in. People, eager to read the libel for themselves, made space to let me pass. I rushed back around the corner into the alley where Master Marlowe waited.

"God's blood, where hast thou been?" he demanded. "Thou couldst have run to St. Paul's and back. Well, what? What does it say?"

Stumbling, I repeated what I could remember of the rhyme. Master Marlowe grew pale as he listened. When I told him what the last lines said, and what the signature had been, he closed his eyes for a moment, looking as young and frightened as Robin.

"They want to kill me," he said shakily, but not as if he spoke to me. "I did not think 'twould come to this."

"Who?" He did not seem to hear me. "Master, what is happening? Did you write that poem?"

"Oh, so thou thinkst so, too?" He was aware of me again, and his voice was savage. "*I* am the one inciting every idle apprentice and layabout beggar in London to bloody riot?"

"'Tis a forgery," I realized. "Someone else put the name of Tamburlaine to it."

"God's teeth, of *course* 'tis a forgery," he snapped. "Thinkst thou I could rhyme as ill as that, even if I tried?"

"But someone meant—"

"For pity's sake, peace. Aye, someone meant everyone who saw that to think I am a bloodthirsty murdermonger. And now, if there's a riot, who'll be blamed?" He ran both hands through his hair, as if trying to force his thoughts back inside his skull. "I must—I must out of London. Richard. Get thee to my rooms, pack my clothes." He put out a hand to forestall the questions he saw gathering in my face. "*Now*, Richard!"

As I ran toward Master Marlowe's lodgings, one ridiculously simple thought squirmed free from the confusion and bewilderment seething in my brain. If Master Marlowe were determined to go on a journey, at least his collar and cuffs were clean.

Master Marlowe left London that afternoon. For the country, he said, I did not need to know where, and I was to tell anyone who asked that he had been there two weeks at the least. He tossed a handful of coins on the table for the rent and my keep, snatched up the bag I had packed with his belongings, and was gone, his heels clattering down the steps.

There was no riot after all, though stories drifted in

and out of Mistress Stavesly's shop with the customers—a Dutchman had been killed, or had killed two Englishmen, or had only been threatened; a shop had been burned, or perhaps only plundered, the goods taken or broken. No one seemed to know which tales were true, if any, and I certainly did not dare set foot in the Dutch neighborhood to find out for myself.

There was little for me to do. I kept Master Marlowe's lodgings clean, and went on errands for Mistress Stavesly, and taught Moll to play simple games, winding string into patterns around our fingers. The sky was fresh and blue, the breezes sweet with spring, but to me the air in the city seemed dense and close. It pressed on my lungs, making it hard to breathe. No one else seemed to notice it, but I could not rid myself of the sense of a coming storm.

It had nothing to do with me, I reminded myself often. Master Marlowe had warned me. I had obeyed. His troubles, his white, frightened face, were none of my affair.

Master Marlowe had been gone perhaps a week when I saw a second libel, pasted up on the wall of a grocer's. The shopkeeper was scraping it off, to the indignation of those who had not read it yet.

Across the street, I hesitated. I wanted to know what the libel said, if it were another forgery set to blame Master Marlowe. But I was not far from Bishopsgate;

anyone in this crowd might know me for my master's servant. I tugged my hat down lower over my face, just as a dark-haired, thin-faced man on the edge of the crowd caught my attention. Surely I had seen him before. Then I remembered. Master Marlowe had laughed at him. *A few coins to clink in thy purse and thou canst afford to cast off old friends,* he'd said. What had his name been? Thomas Kyd?

Kyd turned his back on the crowd, walking away from the scene and passing someone else I knew. My heart lightened at the sight of a tall, lanky figure with tousled yellow hair, and I hurried across the street to tug on Will's shoulder. "Will! Did you read it?"

"Richard!" Will turned around with a start that seemed almost guilty, clutching at the basket he carried over one arm. "Come away from this."

"Nay, take yourselves off!" the grocer was scolding the watchers as Will put a hand on my arm and drew me down the street. "You'll keep my customers away. Have you no homes to go to?"

"What did it say?" I asked Will anxiously.

"The same as the others," he answered.

"Others?"

"Aye, 'tis the third I've seen myself. Good that he's taking it down. The city does not need such poison."

I dreaded to ask, and yet I needed to know. "Was it . . . signed?"

"Nay, of course not. Who would sign such a thing as that?"

I sighed with relief. Not "Tamburlaine," then. Maybe these libels were not, after all, meant as an attack on my master. Maybe the mention of his plays had been coincidence, no more.

"Leave that be!" The grocer's angry voice rang out in the street behind us.

We stopped and turned in surprise to see a skinny young man in a patched doublet running with a torn and ragged piece of paper in his hand. He was looking back over his shoulder at the grocer and so did not see Will and me until he had plowed straight into us, sending all three of us sprawling into the gutter.

The stranger did not lose a moment, but scrambled to his feet again. "'Tis truth!" he shouted, waving his fragment of the libel defiantly, as if it were a weapon or a banner. "You cannot silence it!" And he took to his heels. The grocer was not inclined to chase him farther and leave his shop unattended, so he was in little danger.

Will, on his hands and knees, was scrambling to pick up the contents of his basket before his belongings could be kicked aside or trampled into the mud. I hurried to help him and found myself holding a pair of rough wool breeches, loose at the knee, such as a sailor might wear.

"The city's gone mad," Will grumbled, snatching a brimless wool cap off the cobblestones. "As though we had no troubles before the Dutch came here. As though—" He stopped, seeing what I held, and looked at me, a bit shamefaced.

Silently I handed the breeches to him, and he stowed them away in his basket and got to his feet, helping me up as well.

The warmth of his skin against mine seemed to spread from my hand up through my arm and shoulder and wrap itself around my heart.

The Swallow *has need of a new crew . . . When she sails again in the spring . . .*

"Now?" I asked, my voice feeble. "Your ship, is she . . . ?"

"Soon. A week or two. You'll not tell my father?"

"You know I will not."

"Aye. I know well."

"Will—," I said helplessly. There must be some argument to convince him of the folly of what he planned. If I were wise enough, I could find the words to touch his heart and change his mind.

"I know you do not approve, Richard," he said. "But

you'll keep faith. I wish I could make you understand. I *cannot* stay."

I could only look at him, silent, tears stinging my eyes. I knew that if I tried to speak, my voice would betray my own secret.

"Richard?"

I was so tired of secrets. I was weary of things I could not tell. The pressure of all the unspoken words in my throat came near to choking me. Suddenly I raised myself on my toes and let my lips press against the skin of his cheek, just to one side of his mouth.

"God keep thee safe," I whispered, and fled.

In the moment before I turned away, I saw his hand go up to touch his face, and his eyebrows drew together in a frown—puzzled, disapproving, surprised, angry? I could not wait to see. I was running, my feet slipping on cobblestones, darting around pedestrians and horses and carts, moving quickly enough to vanish in the crowd.

I had more or less stopped weeping by the time I'd reached Mistress Stavesly's bakery again. "Nay, I know not," she was saying as I tried to slip by unnoticed. "But here's his boy; he'll know. Richard!"

Praying that my eyes were not red nor my face marked with tears, I turned to her. "Yes, mistress?"

"This gentleman needs to speak with thy master," she

238 Sarah L. Thomson

said, nodding at a man with kindly dark eyes beneath a red velvet hat that bore a floating white plume.

My heart stuttered to a stop, then jerked back into life.

"Indeed, I have important news for him," Pooley said, formal and polite.

"He's left London," I said rapidly. "Three weeks since." It was the second time I'd lied for my master, but that did not cross my mind at the moment. I was only eager to give this man whatever answers he wanted so that he would leave.

I saw Mistress Stavesly's frown, and Pooley saw it, too.

"Three weeks?" he said and looked toward her. "Did you not say he had been gone fourteen days?"

Thou'rt a clumsy liar, Richard, my master's voice whispered in my mind. But Mistress Stavesly was more skilled.

"Two weeks, three, I care not," she said indifferently. "He's but my lodger. So long as the rent is paid, I do not mark his comings and goings. I've bread in the oven, if you'll pardon me." And she walked back to the kitchens, leaving me and Pooley alone.

"Dost know when he'll return?" Pooley asked me. I shook my head. Since I could not lie without tripping over my tongue, it would be best not to speak at all if I could help it.

"Canst take a message to him?" Again I shook my head.

But Pooley did not seem exasperated. He smiled at me, and with a hand on my shoulder drew me over near the staircase. He bent down, his voice for my ears only.

"There are those who would speak with your master," he told me. "He may hide in Kent only so long—oh, aye, I know well enough where he is." He almost seemed amused, but then his face became serious. "I am watched; I dare not go to him myself. But he has need of a friend, dost understand? And 'twould be best if he came back of his own will. Tell him so."

"I know not where he is," I protested. "He did not tell me—"

"A loyal heart thou hast," Pooley said with approval, and looked as if he felt sorry for me. "But thou'rt too young to be worried in this. Thy master should not have involved thee in his affairs."

He had not. He'd warned me. I had tried hard to know nothing.

"Tell him what I've told you," Pooley said. "For thy pains." He laid a bright silver penny in my hand.

"Master, please." I held the coin out to him again. "I cannot bear your message. I do not know where Master Marlowe has gone."

Pooley chuckled indulgently, straightened his hat, and left me there, clutching his money tightly in my hand.

chapter sixteen
may 1593

❧

I had no way of sending Pooley's warning to my master, and no way of knowing if it was truly best that he should come back to London. But without my intervention, fifteen days after he had gone, Master Marlowe returned.

I was in the bakery, helping Mistress Stavesly take loaves of bread out of the oven. The smell of them, rich and yeasty, rose around us. After the bread was safely displayed on the counter, Mistress Stavesly would cut open a loaf and give a slice each to me and Moll, spreading it with her currant jam. My mouth was watering already, thinking of that warm, soft mouthful and the tart-sweet tang of the currants.

Master Marlowe must have stood for some time in the doorway, watching us. He did not make a sound. It was only as I turned that I caught sight of him, his face pale in contrast to his black doublet, leaning with one shoulder against the doorjamb, as if he were too tired to stand without support.

I nearly let a loaf of bread slip off the long-handled wooden paddle I was using to slide it from the oven. I had to juggle it like an acrobat at the summer fairs, and barely managed to drop it on the table rather than the floor. Mistress Stavesly turned swiftly, her floury skirts swinging, only to stand as still as Master Marlowe. But while he seemed merely tired, she looked alert, as if she were waiting for something to happen.

Master Marlowe smiled very slightly at my awkwardness, a twitch that stirred only one corner of his mouth. "Good day to you both," he said quietly.

Mistress Stavesly inclined her head, just a little. "Good day, Master Marlowe," she said, as if she had seen him only yesterday.

"I do not need Richard at the moment," Master Marlowe told her. "You're welcome to keep him, if he is of any use to you." He did not look at me.

Mistress Stavesly nodded. "Thank you," she answered. "He's a handy boy. I do find him useful."

"Aye, Richard knows how to make himself helpful," Master Marlowe said, still in that strange, dull, tired voice. And that was all that passed between them. Simple, quiet, passionless words. I did not understand, then, why the air in the kitchen felt so weighted down that it seemed the dough would never rise.

When a little later I made my way up to Master Marlowe's rooms, I found him seated at the table, scribbling away, as if he had never been gone. I stood hesitantly in the doorway. He paused to dip the pen in the ink, looked up, and noticed me.

"Is . . . is all well, Master?" I asked awkwardly. He dropped his eyes to the paper again. "I did not think to see you back so soon."

"Nor did I think to be here." Carefully, deliberately, he dipped the pen deep and scored a heavy black mark through the last five or six lines he had written. "But I received an invitation that 'twas difficult to refuse."

I could simply go into his room, unpack his bag, and ask him nothing. That, surely, was what our arrangement called for. He had warned me not to ask, not to listen, not to know.

And I had tried. I'd done my best to be deaf and blind. But I knew things now that I had not wanted to learn, and yet I could not forget them.

I heard Master Marlowe's voice in my mind: *They want to kill me. I did not think 'twould come to this.*

And behind his voice was another, soft and tender

as an echo: *Do not trust him to keep you from having your conscience scraped clean.* . . .

I knew my master was in danger. I knew he was in peril of his life. And it was well enough for Mistress Stavesly to ask for the rent and nothing else. She could say she knew no more of him than the coins he put into her hand each week. But I was his servant, part of his household. No one would believe that I knew nothing of his affairs. Pooley had shown me that. Any trouble Master Marlowe was in would likely fall on me as well.

So I did not go into the bedchamber to unpack his clothes. I deliberately disobeyed him and asked a question.

"An invitation?"

He did not lift his eyes from the page he was writing, but he answered me.

"Aye, an invitation. The kind a sheriff comes to deliver."

There are those who would speak with your master. . . .

"You were arrested?" I whispered.

He nodded. "Do not look so shocked." With a sigh, he laid down the pen and rubbed his eyes as if they ached with weariness. "'Tis over. They let me go. They will not touch me now."

"They?" I asked weakly. My tongue felt stiff at the roots.

"I've had enough of questions for today, Richard." He ran both hands through his hair, pulling it together at the nape of his neck. "'Tis over now, that is all thou needst to understand. Go and unpack for me. And then take thyself to the tavern. I'm parched for some ale. Two days' talking is thirsty work."

It was over, so he said. He believed it. The last time I had seen him, he had vibrated with fear like a lute string, plucked and quivering. And now he was still. He sat quietly, moved slowly. It was not quite peace. But it was no longer that jagged energy of fear that had chased him out of the city two weeks ago.

He believed it was over. But he was wrong.

Some days later he sent me to the market for pens and ink. I was climbing the stairs with my purchases in my basket when I heard, beyond the door, voices raised.

This time I did not hesitate to listen. I had been climbing slowly and my shoes were soft soled. The voices did not pause when I halted my steps.

Master Marlowe spoke first. "No. No, it cannot be. I answered every question. They released me."

And the second voice, smooth, soft, gentle. "Do not be such a fool, Kit. You know they can take you up again as easily as they let you go."

"But I had naught to do with that libel. You know it, Pooley. They know it."

"'Tis not the libel anymore."

"That accusation Kyd made? 'Tis nothing, 'tis foolishness. He was talking to save his own skin."

"'Tis nothing Kyd said anymore, either. Have some sense and listen!" A pause. "The libel, Kyd's words—they were nothing but the bait. Once the hook is fairly in your jaw, they'll reel you in and spend a few days finding out what you know. Or what you can be compelled to say. Then, if they don't hang you, they might let you go. Perhaps you'll even be able to walk again afterward. You know it, Kit, well enough. You know what they will do."

"I have friends who will speak for me," Master Marlowe snapped.

"For pity's sake, Kit. Your most faithful patron just spent two years in the Tower. Think you his word has any weight these days?"

"I will use what I know," Master Marlowe said. It should have been a threat. But it sounded more like a plea.

"'Twas your faith in what you know that brought you to this pass," Pooley said regretfully. "It did not save Watson, and 'twill not save you. I warned thee, Kit. I warned thee not to cross the hunchback." Pooley sounded like a grieved father and, like a father, used the tender "thou." "Why wouldst thou not listen to me?"

"I have done good service," Master Marlowe said, more weakly still. "How many Catholic plots have I told him of? How many priests did I deliver to him?"

"And think you that matters now?" Pooley sighed. "A playmaker, a cobbler's son, and you dared to match wits with the hunchback. Did you forget what you are? Men like us, common men, we serve their turn and are lucky if we keep our skins whole."

"I'll give him the letter," Master Marlowe offered. Suddenly all his defiance was gone, melted like hot wax. "I'll give it to him, Pooley. You'll tell him for me."

"'Tis not just the letter," Pooley answered gently. "Thou hast offended him, Kit. One of his own spies with the nerve to leave his service? To threaten him? 'Tis very ill, I will not hide it from thee."

There was a long silence. When at last Master Marlowe spoke again, he sounded like a guilty child.

"What shall I do, Robin?"

"There is one chance." Pooley sounded businesslike now. "You cannot stay in London, under his nose. He'll see it as defiance."

"I'll go back to Canterbury," Master Marlowe offered eagerly.

"Think you his arm does not reach so far as Canterbury? No, Kit, you must leave the country, and soon. Waste no time. Tomorrow."

"Tomorrow?" Master Marlowe sounded dazed. "I cannot get a passage so quickly."

"I know a ship. I can arrange it," Pooley said briskly. "The captain has carried passengers for me before. He'll ask no questions. Tomorrow, Kit. I'll come for you in the morning. Bring the letter with you. When you're gone, I'll take it to the hunchback. Once he has it in his hands, and you far away, he may let the matter rest. Trust me, Kit. 'Twill be for the best."

I heard the legs of the stool scrape across the floor, and realized that the conference was at an end. Swiftly and silently, I crept back down the stairs and waited outside, well hidden around a corner of the house, until I saw Pooley leave.

If Master Marlowe wondered at the time I had taken fetching his pens and ink, he did not mention it to me. In fact, he barely spoke to me that day.

My master was not an atheist, I thought as I lay under the blankets that night. He was not a witch or a conjuror. He was certainly not a secret Catholic.

He was a spy.

An intelligencer. A listener to other men's secrets. The

eyes and ears that reported dangers to the men who worked for the queen. Dangers like secret Catholics. Like my father, my brother. Like me.

But he knew. He knew what I was; he had known it for months. And I was not in prison, nor was Robin. If he knew, why had he not accused us? Why were we still free?

And tomorrow he would be gone. Well, good riddance to him. Informer, telltale, vulture. Telling the world that Catholics were bloodthirsty murderers, our knives whetted for Protestant throats, when all the while he was the one betraying his neighbors to the prison, the rope, the rack.

But he had not so betrayed me.

I spent that night in a state of bitter confusion, and it was no better in the morning. Master Marlowe did not seem surprised that I asked no questions as I packed his belongings once again, his extra shirts, his old doublet, a spare pair of breeches, the tinderbox, his razor and comb and scissors. Carefully I rolled up the manuscript of the new play and tied it with cord. Ink and pens and penknife went into a small wooden case that locked shut to keep them safe. All of Master Marlowe's life, it seemed, fit neatly into a leather satchel that he could carry over one shoulder.

"All prepared, then, Kit?" Pooley was standing in the open doorway.

"In a moment," Master Marlowe said quietly. He seemed unsurprised, though Pooley must have come up the stairs as quietly as a cat stalking a mouse. "Wait for me outside, I pray. I will not be long."

There was something in his manner that made me think of the knight who had appeared at the playhouse when *The Massacre at Paris* had first been performed. And Pooley seemed to feel it, too, for he turned obediently and made his way downstairs, for all the world as if Master Marlowe, a playmaker, a cobbler's son, had the right to give him orders and to be obeyed.

Master Marlowe had his sword at his side. He wore the same magnificent black doublet he was wearing when I saw him first, the gilt buttons shining like small moons. But his face above it was worn and white, as if his sleep had been hagridden for many nights. It was not a face that went with his rich man's clothes.

Out of a purse at his belt he drew a handful of coins and laid them on the table. "Pay Mistress Stavesly the rent for this week," he said quietly. And then another handful rang softly as he laid them beside the first. "A quarter's wages for thee. I am sorry to break our contract, but I must go."

I nodded, but I couldn't keep my eyes from widening. I had not expected such generosity from him.

"And here." From inside his doublet he drew a folded piece of paper. "Keep this for me, until I am well gone."

My eyes fell on a dark brown stain, the size of a shilling, on the top right corner of the paper.

"No!" I flinched back, as if the letter were contaminated with plague. "No, master, please, do not ask me."

"'Sblood, take it," Master Marlowe said, suddenly angry. He took a step toward me. "Take it and do not read it. If all goes well and I get safely away, burn it unopened. If not, I will return for it. 'Twill do thee no harm."

How could he say so? I was fairly sure that this letter had been the cause of Tom Watson's death. Master Marlowe must flee the country because of it. And now he would hand it to me?

"I will not touch it!" I said, more sharply than I had ever dared to speak to him. But he had broken our contract. He was my master no longer. Aware that ears might be listening, I lowered my voice and hissed at him, "You told me to close my eyes, stop my ears, and forget all I heard. I have done it. I'll have no part of your spy's business!"

In the hush that followed my words, I heard the floorboards creak under Master Marlowe's feet. I heard Mistress Stavesly, downstairs, call out, "Moll!" I heard a laden cart clatter its way over the street outside.

"Bright lad," Master Marlowe said at last. "Dost know so much? Then dost know this—what I am facing?" He did not move toward me, but I felt as if he had, his eyes were so fierce on my face. "Dost know what the rack will do to a man? How it will take every bone from its socket? They put a stone under the spine, to make it worse. Or perhaps they will only hang me by my wrists and leave me until my own weight pulls my joints apart."

I was silenced, but I still shook my head when he held the letter out again toward me.

"Do not cross me." There was a clear warning in his voice. "Thou'rt not so safe thyself. A young Catholic, a worm at the heart of the state, a plotter and contriver. I could tell them of thee."

Anger had stiffened my spine, but now fear weakened me again. "Master, please," I whispered, searching his face for a hint of pity and finding none.

"Oh, I could tell them. A Catholic traitor, dressed in boy's clothing, blasphemous and shameless. Who knows what other secrets she may be hiding? She may be a spy for Spain, or for Rome. She may even be a witch."

He laughed harshly at the look on my face.

"Didst take me for a fool? Didst think I would not notice that my servant boy had a cheek smooth as an apple and a voice that never cracked? When I see boys in women's skirts every day, didst think a baggage in breeches could hoodwink me?" Now he did take a step toward me, holding the letter as a thief might hold a knife. "Mind well. They'll only lock thee up for a papist. But they'll burn thee alive for a witch."

It was not true. He was only trying to frighten me. The law would punish me, if they found out I was disguised. But they would not burn me, just for my breeches . . . would they?

I had moved away from him, and the wall was at my back. I felt as if I were pinned there. The force of his threats seemed to fill up the room.

I remembered something he had said on the day I met him.

"You said the devil walks like a man," I choked out. "You said he gets souls by whispering." And sweet saints, it was true. I had thought my brother and I were only doing what we must to save our lives. I had thought there was no sin in that. But it was possible to pay too high a price for safety.

Faustus had traded his soul to the devil in return for pleasure and riches. What had I traded to this man when I promised to brush his clothes, carry his messages, and keep his secrets? I should have gone to prison alongside my father before I'd accepted his help. I should have starved on the streets of London. But now it was too late to repent.

They'll burn thee alive for a witch. I knew I did not have the courage to face what the law might do to me if Master Marlowe betrayed me. With the taste of my cowardice sour in my mouth, I held out a hand for the letter.

But Master Marlowe did not hand it to me. He looked stricken. And suddenly his rage, that had seemed to push all the air into the corners of the room, was gone. I felt as if we had both shrunk to half our former size.

"Oh, well played." He said it lightly, but he closed his eyes briefly as he spoke, as if he were mortally wounded. "Who taught thee to turn a man's own words against him?"

I only stared in confusion.

"When I said that, I did not think of *myself. . . .*" He shook his head. "Pardon, Richard—no. What is thy name?"

"Rosalind," I said shakily.

"Thy pardon, Rosalind. I would not—" He sighed. "I *will* not betray thee. 'Twas my fear speaking. All that blood spilled on the stage to hide the fact that I am a coward at last." As if he were too tired to stand, he sank down on the stool beside the table and looked up at me beseechingly. "I will only ask thee, beg thee, take the letter. I dare not destroy it yet. I must trust this man, 'tis my only hope, but he may not . . . That letter may well be my only safety." He shuddered. "I cannot face it, what they will do to me. 'Tis wrong to bring thee into this, I know. But I have no other recourse. I do not ask it of thy love, but only of thy pity. If nothing else, that letter may buy me a quick death."

Changeable as March wind. He had threatened me with exposure and death, but he had saved me from beggary. Just now, he may as well have held a knife to my throat. But he had comforted me on the day I learned my father was dead.

Now he asked for my pity. And he held my secret like an eggshell in the palm of his hand.

I did pity him. I could not help it, seeing the fear that shook him. Even so, I could not forget the power he had over me. *Changeable as March wind.* He had said he would not force the letter on me, that he would not betray me. But that did not blot out what he could do to me, to Robin, if he changed his mind.

I held out a hand that trembled only slightly.

To my surprise, Master Marlowe did not simply give the letter to me. Instead, he slipped from his stool and in one quick movement was kneeling at my feet. He placed the letter between my fingers and then, as if I were the queen herself, he lifted my hand to his lips and kissed it gently. And when he spoke to me again, he did not use the "thou" a master uses to his servant. For the first time, he called me "you," as if I were his equal.

"You were to redeem me, Rich—Rosalind. Did you know that? I thought, two young papists, no threat to England. So many as I have betrayed, these two perhaps I can save." He rose to his feet. "It seems I have no talent for redemption. If you hear nothing of me by tomorrow, burn that letter. And 'twill all be at an end."

He picked up the leather bag, slung it over his shoulder, and left the room, closing the door quietly behind him.

may 1593

❧

The day went past with no word, and when I woke from an uneasy sleep the next morning, I felt the sharpest edge of my fear beginning to melt away. Surely Master Marlowe was safely on board a ship by now, out of sight of England's shore. Which meant that I could strike a spark and set fire to the letter, and be free of all the toils and tangles of my old master and his secrets.

Strike a spark—aye, there was the problem. Master Marlowe, naturally, had taken the tinderbox with him, so there was no flint and steel in the room. No matter. There were always coals in Mistress Stavesly's oven. I dressed myself quickly, winding the linen bands around my breasts once more and noticing that lately I had been forced to tie the knot closer to the end of the worn cloth. Was it possible that I was not going to be a feather, a sprite, for all of my life?

It was not the moment, however, to worry about it. I fished the letter out from under the edge of my pallet, where I had hidden it next to my rosary while I slept. Yesterday I had cut a slit in the lining of my doublet. I slipped the letter into this pocket, tucked the rosary back into its bag around my neck, and hurried down the stairs.

Mistress Stavesly was already in the kitchen, tying her long white apron around her waist. Dismay clutched at my heart. I could not burn the letter before her.

"Ah, Richard." If she wondered why I was stirring so early, she gave no sign of it. "Just the lad I need. Run to the market for me. I've much to do, and I need a pot of honey and a dozen eggs. Moll will only get cheated if I send her. Go on, lad, and I'll give thee something to break thy fast when thou returnst."

My mouth opened, but I could put no words to my objection. What excuse did I have to refuse to run her errand, so kind as she had always been to me? The letter had been safe enough for all of yesterday, tucked inside my doublet. Another hour could make no difference. And then I would take a moment when her back was turned, or I would find flint and steel myself, and the letter would be no more.

But when I came back, with fresh eggs and a crock of honey in my basket, Mistress Stavesly was not so busy as she had claimed to be. She was sitting quietly on a stool, with her floury hands resting in her lap.

I set the basket down on a table. "Mistress Stavesly?"

There was something on the floor at her feet. Master Marlowe's leather satchel.

"Oh, Richard." Were there tears in her eyes? "Ill news, I am afraid."

"He has returned?" I couldn't take my eyes off the satchel, slouched there on the tile floor. He had not gotten safely away after all. He had not slipped free of the trap.

"No, that he has not." She sighed. "I am sorry, Richard. Thy master is dead."

A constable had come while I was gone, bringing word and Master Marlowe's things. I listened dully to the story she told, of a meal in a victualling house, a quarrel over the reckoning. Master Marlowe had, it seemed, argued with a companion over who was to pay the bill. He'd snatched the man's dagger to slash at him and, in the struggle, gotten the knife in his own eye. So the constable had told Mistress Stavesly, and so she now told me.

"There will be a trial, of course, but 'tis self-defense, no doubt on't." She shook her head. "Far too young. 'Tis always the young ones who die so. Perhaps you must grow old, and see how little life you have left, before you learn to value it. 'Tis a young man's trick, to throw away his life over a few pence."

Whatever Master Marlowe had thrown his life away
over, I was sure it had not been a penny or two for a meal.
I must trust this man, 'tis my only hope, he had said. His
hope and his trust had been false.

"He was a strange one," Mistress Stavesly said mourn-
fully. "You could never be sure if he was speaking in jest.
But he had a kind heart in the end, had he not, Richard?"

A kind heart? He had saved my life and my brother's,
only to drag me into peril when it suited him. I could not
say if this meant he had a kind heart in the end. Still, kind
or cruel, angry or gentle, threatening or pleading, he had
been alive. *Changeable as March wind.* Now that restless
energy, that sharp tongue, that quick mind, were forever
still.

"Mistress Stavesly!" I said abruptly. "The rooms—he
left me money to pay this week's rent. May I stay out the
time?"

She looked oddly at me. Perhaps she thought me
heartless.

"Aye, Richard, of course thou mayst stay the week." A
customer appeared at the window, and she rose to sell him
the loaf he wanted.

I snatched the satchel and ran up the stairs. A corner of
the letter nudged my ribs through my shirt and the lining

of my doublet. The tinderbox was in the satchel; I had packed it there myself. One spark and this would be over. Frantic to put an end to this letter that had caused two men's deaths, I yanked the door to Master Marlowe's lodgings open, only to stop a step or two into the room.

My pallet had been slashed open with a knife, and the stuffing littered the floor. The blanket had been thrown aside. Through the door into Master Marlowe's bedchamber, I could see that his mattress had been treated the same way, heaved off the rope webbing that supported it and slit from seam to seam. The lid of his chest had been thrown open, but there had been little left inside it to dump out. The box Mistress Stavesly had given me to store my few belongings had been overturned, my nightshirt and cloak tossed aside, my store of coins tossed across the floor.

That was not the worst of it, however.

Pooley stood by the bookshelf, looking over one of the books that Master Marlowe had left behind. He carefully thumbed through to the last page, held the book by the spine and shook it, then shrugged and dropped it on the floor by his feet. Only then did he turn and smile at me.

"Shut the door, boy. No need to disturb those below," he said pleasantly.

My knees had locked. Master Marlowe's satchel slipped

out of my hand to the floor. Pooley wore his dark red hat, with the white plume nodding gracefully. The velvet glowed ruby in a shaft of light from the window. It seemed as if the shadow it cast over his face should be bloodred.

When I did not move, he walked past me to shut the door himself. The straw and chaff from the bedding, scattered across the floor, stirred slightly in the wind made by his feet.

He did nothing so obvious as lay a hand on the hilt of the rapier that hung at his belt. He only leaned against the door with folded arms and regarded me. "Richard. How pleasant to see thee once again. Thou canst save me some time and much trouble. Thy master had in his keeping something that belongs to me. Knowst of what I speak?"

He was friendly, reasonable, calm, as if he only asked a favor that any man would grant. My voice was trapped in my throat. Should I deny all knowledge? Should I hand him the letter and let that be the end of it?

"I see thou dost know, or thou wouldst have answered more quickly." But it was not an accusation. His look was sympathetic. "Thou'rt frightened, Richard, and 'tis no wonder. But this is no concern of thine. Thou wast loyal to thy master while he lived, and 'twas a credit to thee. But now—" He smiled gently, sadly, and held out his empty hands, palms up, to show me how little use loyalty could be to Master Marlowe.

"Thy master had a letter of mine," he went on. "'Tis a small thing, but he had no right to it, and I wish it back. Tell me where 'tis, and all will be well. Thou mayst trust me."

I longed to do it, to reach into my doublet and hand him the letter. So simple, so quick. And this deadly thing would be gone, out of my hands.

But—*trust me, Kit.* It was what he had said to Master Marlowe. And Master Marlowe was dead.

"Hast thy tongue shriveled at the root?" An edge of impatience crept into Pooley's tone. "Thy master had a letter of mine. Tell me where 'tis."

"At the playhouse," I blurted out. "He hid it there, he told me so."

"And where, precisely?" Pooley's voice was as gentle as ever. But his chin came up slightly and his eyes narrowed.

"Beneath the stage," I lied. "There is a trapdoor. He hid the letter there. He told me where to find it, if he did not return."

If he would only believe me, would turn and leave the room and give me a respite of some minutes, an hour, so that I could think of what to do. Then I might find a way to rid myself of the letter inside my doublet that seemed to bring death with it wherever it went.

Pooley smiled approvingly, as if I were his pupil and had answered a question satisfactorily. "Excellent. My thanks to thee, Richard. Come, we will go together."

"Together?" I croaked.

"Of course. Thou wishest to help me, dost not, Richard? I can see thou'rt a helpful boy. And they know thee at the Rose, I think. Come, let's be on our way."

He did not take hold of my arm or seize me by the collar. He only opened the door and gestured at me to lead the way. I could feel his presence close on my heels as we went down the stairs and outside into the street. The threat of him pressed heavy on my lungs, cramped my breath. It was a cold, sharp, bitter taste on the back of my tongue. He had killed a gentleman, a well-known playmaker. When he found that I had lied, there would be nothing to keep him from murdering an orphan servant boy.

I did not see my chance until we were crossing Cheapside. Two carts had met in the center of the road, their horses nose to nose, and the two carters stood, shouting at each other. People squeezed past, grumbling. Another cart was making its way east, and would soon add to the confusion. I slowed and hesitated, as if looking for the best way through the tangle. Pooley slowed also, and I took the moment to dive beneath the belly of one of the cart horses, scrambling on hands and knees out the other side.

Horses do not care for such tricks, even placid cart horses bred for strength and not for speed. This one threw up its head and backed a few paces into the cart coming up from behind. There were fresh shouts and curses and I ducked under someone's elbow, knocked aside a basket of eggs, shoved my way between two bodies, saw free ground in front of me again, and ran as if the devil himself were after me. The devil, who gets souls by whispering.

I did not dare pause to look behind, but dodged into the first alley I saw, my feet slipping on muddy cobbles. The second stories of the buildings on either side all but met over my head as I raced down the dark tunnel, around the next corner, and the next, running blindly, like a rabbit across a field, dashing this way and that, doubling back, with the dogs at her heels.

The rabbit, however, might have sense enough to stay out of a dead end.

The alley I had turned into stopped at a wall too high for me to climb. To one side there was a tavern. Perhaps I could dash through the kitchen and out into the street. But no one could fail to notice me, and they would all be able to tell Pooley where I had gone.

I needed a better plan. I needed to disappear.

There was a rubbish heap piled up against the wall—bones, scraps of food, broken crates, empty barrels stacked two high. If I climbed to the topmost barrel, I might be able to scramble over the wall.

I seized the highest barrel and gave it a shove with all my strength. It tottered for a moment, then fell to the cobbled street with a crash that rang and echoed like the fall of a hundred-year-old oak. I dove for the far side of the rubbish heap, pushed aside an empty crate, and crawled between it and the wall. I yanked another crate over me and then froze at the sound of running footsteps.

"What the devil is happening?" The loud, angry voice had a thick country accent.

"Have you seen a boy run past?" This voice was Pooley's, and his breath heaved. "He stole my purse. I know he turned in here." I pressed myself as small and still against the ground as I could, praying that Pooley would notice the toppled barrel and would think I had kicked it as I climbed over the wall. The smell of the garbage was overwhelming, and someone had been using this alley as a privy. The stench clung to my nostrils and the inside of my throat.

"Nay, I've seen no boy. Look there! Who's been knocking my barrels about?"

"Damnation," muttered Pooley, and this must have been followed by more blasphemy, for the tavern keeper intervened.

"No call for such language, master. Tell the law, if a thief has taken what's yours. Will you come inside for a glass of something? 'Twill do you good."

"Hell with it. And you!" Pooley snapped, and his footsteps retreated down the alleyway. But I stayed where I was, unmoving, until I heard the tavern keeper set the barrel back upright, muttering under his breath. Even when he returned to his tavern, I didn't dare move. Suppose Pooley had guessed? Suppose he had walked silently back and now stood waiting for me to emerge from my filthy hiding place?

I held my breath, listening, and heard nothing—no quiet breathing, no feet shifting on cobblestones. Only a scratching, skittering noise of tiny claws. Rats usually forage at night, but for such a treasure trove as this, sunlight would not stop them. Something soft and furry tickled my arm, and I choked back a cry and scrambled out, my skin prickling with horror. Pooley was not there.

I had escaped, for the moment. But it did not take much thought for me to realize that it couldn't be for long.

I had nowhere to go. I had no money in my purse. My

small hoard of coins lay scattered over the floor of Master Marlowe's room. I had nothing but the clothes on my back and Master Marlowe's deadly letter, which felt as if it were slowly singeing the cloth of my doublet and shirt. Soon it would burn a hole clean through and I would have nowhere to hide.

That was what I needed, somewhere to hide. But where? It might take Pooley some time to find one boy in all the crowds of London, but I was fairly sure he would do it at last. The letter was obviously important to him; he would not rest until he had it back.

I could burn it, lose it, drop it in the Thames. But now I understood better Master Marlowe's reluctance to destroy it. As long as I had the letter and Pooley did not, he did not dare kill me.

He could make my life most unpleasant, however. *Dost know this—what I am facing?* Master Marlowe's voice sounded in my ear and I shuddered. To keep the letter was to cling to life, but a life that might not be worth living. To hand it over, however, would be inviting death. Pooley knew I was Master Marlowe's servant and clerk; he therefore knew I was lettered. He would never believe that I had left the letter unopened and unread.

She must be silenced, Master Marlowe had said to Master Shakespeare, *else she'll tell all she knows.* Surely, once Pooley had the letter in his hands, disposing of Master Marlowe's inconveniently knowledgeable servant boy would be his very next task.

I had dodged Pooley once by running to earth, like that rabbit dashing into her burrow. But this was only a brief respite. Now I needed something more. If I were to keep myself safe for good, I needed to manage it so that, no matter how hard he looked, Pooley would never find a boy named Richard Archer.

And the thought lit sparks under my heels. I set off running for London Bridge.

chapter eighteen
may 1593

When I arrived at the Rose, I was so out of breath that I had to pause, with my hands on my knees, to gasp and wheeze until I was able to stand upright again. My whole plan, if I could call it that, depended on Pooley believing I had told the truth about the letter, that it was hidden in the playhouse. But it also depended on my reaching the playhouse before he did.

Luckily I knew my way. Six months ago I could barely tell north from south in the maze of London streets. But it had been a rare day that Master Marlowe had not sent me to the Rose on some errand or other. Now I knew every street, every alley, every shortcut. I could only pray that my knowledge and my desperate speed would be enough.

I did not see Pooley anywhere. He might, of course, have hidden himself somewhere to watch the playhouse entrance. I could not wait; I would have to take the risk.

"Ah, Richard," John said as I approached. "Ill news, about thy master, indeed—" I did not stay to hear him finish.

Onstage a fencing lesson was taking place. Nat and Sander were battling back and forth across the boards, rapiers whistling, while Master Cowley shouted out praise and corrections and the other apprentices watched from the yard.

"Good, excellent, Sander. Nat, mind thy feet! Better. Now, Sander, strike at his head—"

"*Ow!*" Nat dropped his sword to ring and clatter on the wooden stage. "Thou pig, thou slicedst off mine *ear*!"

Since he had a hand clapped to the side of his head, no one could tell if this was actually true. But they all crowded around to see, and that gave me a chance to snatch at Robin's arm.

He jumped nearly out of his skin. "*Richard?* What dost here? We heard of Master Marlowe—"

"No time," I hissed in his ear. "Come, I need thy help. Backstage. *Please.*"

Master Cowley was fussing over Nat, who had taken away his hand to show a trickle of blood running down his neck, though his ear still looked to be firmly attached to his head. Sander was stammering apologies. No one noticed as Robin and I ducked backstage.

"What is't?" Robin asked, worried. "Thou lookst terrible. And—" He wrinkled his nose. "Hast been crawling in a trash heap?"

"Yes!" I snapped. My stomach was in a boil with anxiety, my throat and lungs still aching from my wild dash through London. "Robin, listen. I need thee to get Master Green away from the tireroom. Now, this instant. No, do not question me; I'll tell thee after. Just do it. Please."

Saints bless my little brother, he saved me. Quickly, without one more question, he led me to the tireroom. "Wait here," he whispered, and opened the door to stick his head in.

"Master Green, Master Edmont sent me for you. He says his new doublet does not fit and that the color is wrong for his skin."

"Tell Master Edmont to come here and say this to me himself," said Master Green from inside the room. I closed my eyes in silent agony.

"Master Henslowe said that you're to go and see him," Robin improvised. "I left him in the galleries."

"Oh, well enough." Master Green emerged, carrying a length of purple velvet over one arm. "My layabout of a son is nowhere to be found, and now I am sent to follow after foolish players and minister to their vanity. But I will not be to blame when the apparel for Master Achelley's play is unfinished, tell Master Henslowe that." I squeezed myself into the shadows behind Robin. Master Green did not look my way, but stalked down the hall, grumbling.

Robin looked at me anxiously. "I'd best see that he does not meet with Master Edmont, or 'twill all be for naught."

He was risking a beating for my sake, and I knew it, but thanks would have to come later. "Go," I whispered, and slipped into the tireroom, shutting the door behind me.

Cloaks and doublets and gowns, silks and velvets and lace, scarlet, emerald, russet gold, midnight blue. For the first time, the richness of cloth and color gave me no joy. Had these players never heard of *plain* clothing? The last thing I needed was a magnificent dress to call attention to myself. I threw open a chest, looking for simpler garments. Doublets and hose. I tried another. A black mantle, a pair of green sleeves. And at the bottom, a plain brown woolen skirt, such as a servant might wear, with a bodice and sleeves beneath it.

My heartbeat seemed to shake my body, as if I were a drum being beaten from the inside. I paused a moment to listen for Master Green's voice, or the sound of footsteps outside, but heard nothing.

I pulled my doublet over my head and kicked off my breeches. Still no sound from outside. My hands trembled as I wrenched at the strips of linen wound around my chest, at last loosening them enough to drop them to the floor. The bodice, when I pulled it on, was a trifle snug, and I could barely draw breath once I had laced it up. All to the good. I thought back to morning, when I'd noticed the difference in my figure. My hands shook as I clumsily tied the points that held the skirts and the sleeves to the bodice.

Now, my head. A third chest yielded a store of coifs. I tied one quickly over my cropped hair, licking my hands to moisten stray strands and tucking them under the white linen. Then I kicked my breeches behind one of the chests, picked up my doublet, and drew out the letter.

I hesitated. My plan was risky enough already, and I had no time to waste. Master Green might return at any moment. Pooley might be at the playhouse already.

But this letter had brought me into peril of my life. I could hardly be in worse danger than I was now. Since I was to suffer the penalty, I thought I might as well commit the crime.

The paper crackled in my hands. It was still warm from the heat of my skin, the wax seal soft as flesh. I unfolded it and read.

Or, I would have read, had the writing been anything I recognized. The paper was covered with strange symbols—

a cross, a star, a scrawl like a range of mountains. I remembered the paper covered with such symbols that I had once seen on Master Marlowe's table. I had thought it was an incantation, a conjuror's spell. But it had only been, like this, a code.

Beneath each symbol someone had carefully written, in neat, thin printing, a word. Someone had broken this code. It was not Master Marlowe's careless, heavy hand. Was it Tom Watson's writing? Someone else's? How many hands had this letter passed through?

I brought the paper closer to my eyes, so that I could read the small, precise words. The letter was not Pooley's after all, although he had claimed it so. It was a letter from Robert Cecil. And he wrote to James, King of Scotland.

My eye skipped about from sentence to sentence.

I believe and trust you to be the rightful heir to our dear and precious sovereign. . . . I do herein truly and religiously profess that I offer my service and loyalty to Your Majesty. . . . Let Your Highness have patience and be ruled by my advice, and you shall in time come to rule England.

Robert Cecil, who had been to Master Marlowe's play, who was the queen's right hand. Who had a twisted spine and one shoulder higher than the other. *I warned thee not to cross the hunchback,* Pooley had told Master Marlowe. Robert the devil. *The devil gets souls by whispering.*

Master Marlowe had said that Elizabeth refused to name an heir, for fear that her subjects' loyalty would flow, like a diverted stream, to her successor. What would she think if she knew that her most trusted servant had written to a claimant for her throne, promising his service? What would this mean to a queen so quick in jealousy that she jailed her favorite simply for marrying? Elizabeth would not tolerate a divided devotion. No wonder Robert Cecil had killed to have this letter back.

I wished now that I had not read it, that I did not know the true deadliness of what I held. It had been bad enough to think it was a letter of Pooley's. But Robert Cecil, the queen's councilor—he was the one behind it all. Pooley was just his hound. It was Robert Cecil who was the master of the hunt.

There was no time to think of it, no time to let fear clog up my brains. I opened the tireroom door and looked around. Master Green was nowhere in sight. Quickly I slipped out.

The fencing lesson was back in full force onstage. I did not dare look up to see if Robin was there. People were in and out of the playhouse all day, running errands, carrying messages. With luck and God's mercy no one would notice me.

I had forgotten how it felt to have the weight of skirts

around my ankles. I nearly tripped more than once before I remembered to take smaller steps. The coif around my face helped to shadow my features, for which I was grateful, but it cut off my vision to the sides as well. I looked modestly down at the ground before me, and wondered if my skirts would tangle my feet, should I need to run.

At the playhouse door, Pooley was speaking with John.

I felt as if my heart were a knot that had been yanked tight. But I made myself keep walking.

"No strangers during rehearsals," John was saying. But his attention was on Pooley's hand, on the flash of silver between his fingers.

"Simply an errand," Pooley said persuasively. "A message for a friend. 'Twill only be a moment."

"No harm, I suppose," John mumbled. Neither of them glanced at me as I slipped by.

I was tempted to keep walking. Pooley could search the whole playhouse for Richard Archer and never find him. But the letter was in my hand. Walking away from Pooley now would not settle the matter, only postpone it. I turned and touched Pooley on the arm, and moved a few steps aside to draw him away from John.

"Master?" I remembered to curtsey and not bow my head as he turned to me, though my knees felt stiff, out of practice. And I tried to lose the hints of a London accent that my voice had acquired over the past months. I wanted to look and sound like a simple country girl. "A boy gave me this for you. He said 'twas yours by right." With another little bob, I held the letter out to him.

Pooley did not snatch at the letter, but took it slowly. I did not raise my eyes to his face, but only as high as the base of his throat. I saw him swallow.

His gaze felt substantial; I could almost feel it brushing, like a feather, over my skin. This could so easily go wrong. He only needed to reach out and pull the coif away from my cropped hair, and my disguise would be no more. One quick movement would do it, and I would have no defense.

I could feel the heat rising off his skin. So close.

"And this boy," Pooley said, considering. "Where is he gone to?"

"I know not," I replied, as innocently as I could. "He only said he was in a great hurry and could not stay for you."

He was not looking at my face. I felt his eyes linger on the bare skin above my bodice, on the swell of my hips, every curve made clear by the tight lacing. It was very plain that I was not a boy. Then his eyes went to the letter in his hand.

"The seal is broken," he said sharply. "Hast read this?"

I opened my eyes wide, as if in surprise.

"Marry, sir, I cannot read," I answered.

He tucked the letter safely away inside his doublet and gave me a penny for my trouble before going on his way.

I waited for some time in the streets outside the bakery, to make sure that Pooley was not there, watching for Richard. But I did not see him. I could only hope that he was satisfied to have the letter back and would trouble no more about an insignificant servant boy.

Mistress Stavesly had left on an errand, her basket over her arm, which was all to the good. I did not care to risk my thin disguise on her sharp eyes. Moll was another matter; I did not worry about her simple mind. In fact, she was on her hands and knees, scrubbing a sticky spill of honey off the floor, and did not even notice me as I slipped by on my way upstairs.

Nothing had changed. I knelt, and as quickly as I could, gathered coins up from where they lay scattered across the floor, mixed with the straw and chaff from the bedding. I stuffed it all in my purse.

There was nothing else in the room that belonged to me. The few pieces of clothing were Richard's, not mine. Everything else was Master Marlowe's, and I supposed would be sent home to his family. To the father he had said would not weep for him.

No, that was not quite true. There was one thing more. Master Marlowe's satchel still sat where I had dropped it that morning. I opened it to look inside.

Master Marlowe was not a tidy man, but even he would not have left such a mess as this. His shirts had been stuffed in helter-skelter, to wrinkle and ruin the fine linen. The box holding his writing materials had been opened, and the quills were broken. Luckily, the ink bottle was still firmly stoppered, or the disaster would have been worse. Pooley, of course. Looking for his letter.

The manuscript had been cut loose from its cords, and the crumpled pages were loose inside the bag. I pulled them out and quickly sorted them. Thank heaven, they were all there.

I dared not stay longer. With the manuscript in my hand, I slipped back downstairs. Moll was still scrubbing the floor, but when I stood behind her and cleared my throat, she jumped up.

"Richard!" She smiled broadly. "Why art dressed so? Is't a game?"

And I had thought her too lackwitted to see through my disguise—or rather, to recognize me in my true self. More fool I. It took complexity to lie and plot; it took schemes and plans and strategies. But Moll was simpleminded.

She had at least given me an excuse I could use. "Aye, a game." I smiled at her with affection. "And a secret. Thou canst keep a secret, Moll? Tell no one. Only thou and I must know."

She nodded eagerly. "Aye, Moll can keep a secret."

"Good. Silence, then." I handed her six shillings from the hoard I had gathered up off the floor. "This is for thy mother. Here." I tied it up in a corner of her apron so she would not lose it. There was the rent for the week and two shillings extra for the damaged bedding and the mess upstairs.

"Farewell, Moll." I kissed her cheek lightly. She smelled of butter and honey and strong soap. "Give thy mother my thanks." It was little enough, but I had nothing else to leave.

Walking down the streets of London, I thought that I was back to where I had been nine months ago. I had the clothes on my back and the coins in my purse, and the rosary safely hidden around my neck. And that was all. It was almost as if I had never known Master Marlowe. Except that I had his play in my hand, and a destination in my mind.

• • •

"Master Green?"

I stood in the door to the tireroom. In my hands, neatly folded, were the plain dress and coif I had borrowed earlier that morning. I had squandered most of the money I'd reclaimed from Master Marlowe's lodgings on the simple green gown I wore now and the new coif that covered my hair. It had left me nearly penniless again, but I could hardly appear before Master Green and beg a favor of him while wearing clothing I had stolen from his own stores.

Although, now that I could see Master Green, he did not look very likely to notice what gown I was wearing, or much of anything else. He was sitting on his stool, turned so that the light from the window fell on the blue satin spread across his lap. But he was not sewing. He sat hunched over something he held clasped in both hands.

"Aye, what is't?" His voice was heavy and slow.

"Master Green?" I came into the room and put the brown gown and coif quickly on a handy chest, before he could notice them and ask questions. "What is't? What's wrong?" He had seemed just as usual when I'd glimpsed him an hour ago. What could have happened between then and now?

He hardly glanced at me. "My boy's gone."

"Will's gone?" Shocked, I sat down, without thinking, on a chest opposite to him.

He had done it, then, what he'd told me he would do, months ago, on that winter day by the Thames. He'd been preparing for it the last time I had seen him. He was gone to the New World, to hot green jungles and cannibals and beasts no one had ever seen, leaving his father behind. And leaving me as well.

"I am sorry for it," I said, heartfelt.

"I—I was harsh to him." Although his eyes were dry, Master Green rubbed a hand over his face. "I know it. I thought I could shake this nonsense out of him. I only wanted him here. I wanted him safe."

I had wanted that, too. I had tried to tell Will that his place was at home, with his family and his work, obedient to his master and father. But Will's place was on the deck of a ship. Neither his father nor I had been able to hold him.

Master Green suddenly seemed to become aware that he was speaking to a stranger. Smoothly he slipped what he held in his hand into the purse hanging from his belt, but not before I saw a tail of small wooden beads trailing from his fingers.

Master Green had not simply been grieving when I interrupted him. He had been praying.

My heart gave a thump that was sharp, almost painful. But I knew I could say nothing, make no sign. I could not let him know that I had guessed his secret. He did not yet know me well enough to know that he could trust me.

Master Green cleared his throat. "Well. Aye. What dost thou . . ." His voice trailed off. He looked at my face keenly.

I had spent so long as Richard, shrinking back from any notice, that I had to fight an urge to move aside, to turn my face away. It was hard to remember that, now, I had nothing to hide.

"If you please, master, I am looking for work," I said, meeting his gaze squarely. "I can sew and mend, and I know something of players' apparel. I wish for an apprentice's place."

Master Green was looking at me through narrowed eyes. "The playhouse is not for women," he said slowly. "'Twould be a disgrace." But he spoke as if he were not giving full attention to his own words.

"No disgrace in honest work," I countered. "And there are women who work here. Cleaning the stage—"

"Servants. Not apprentices."

"But if I have the skill—"

I held my breath as he weighed the question. He knew well enough that I had the skill.

"'Twas once a disgrace to be a player," I said as persuasively as I could. "Against the law. But now players perform at court before the queen herself. The world changes."

"Aye." Master Green looked as if the idea were true, but not pleasant to him.

"And my cousin, he has done work for you," I added eagerly. "Richard Archer. He could not stay himself, but he sent his greetings, and told me to seek you."

"Oh, indeed. Richard Archer is thy cousin?" Master Green's voice was dry, and I felt a little heat across my cheeks. "He had an eye for color, that lad. Thou canst work as well as he did for me?"

"Aye, master. I can."

"Well, then." Master Green stood up and folded the blue satin into a neat square. "Henslowe may not be pleased, but my tireroom is mine own." He sighed. "I had thought—I had thought to see my son tireman after me. But the world changes. Aye. What is thy name, lass?"

"Rosalind," I told him. "Rosalind Archer."

"Finish hemming this skirt, then, Rosalind Archer, and I will see how thou dost." He held out the satin, and I reached to take it.

But Master Green paused a moment, looking at my hand. My palm was upward, and he could see the scar that stretched across it. He gave one look at the ugly red mark and placed the cloth in my hand.

"Go on, girl, get to work," he said gruffly. "Thinkst thou there is time to waste?"

"I thank you, master," I said with a full heart. "I am grateful."

"Do thy work well, that's the best thanks," Master Green said, and went out. But his harshness did not worry me. This, I thought, was not a man like Master Marlowe, changeable as March wind. Behind his rough words there lay a promise, and I knew that he would honor it. We would keep each other's secrets.

The sunlight came in the window, touching the bright satin, bringing it to a gleam like calm water over white sand. Maybe the port in which Will's ship would drop anchor would have water just this color. My needle moved quickly in my fingers, leaving behind it a wake of stitches almost too small to be seen, but strong enough to hold.

chapter nineteen
may-june 1593

They buried Master Marlowe in the churchyard at Deptford, near the port where he had planned to set sail and escape his peril forever. There was an inquest on his death, and the man who had held the knife, Frizer by name, was pardoned on the grounds of self-defense. Pooley, of course, was never charged with any crime at all.

I did not go either to the inquest or the burial, for fear of curious eyes. But I went to the graveside once. It is a small church with a green yard; it might almost be in the country, if you pay no mind to the stink of the nearby Thames and the sight of masts and sails towering over the roofs of the riverside buildings.

It is a peaceful place, the graveyard. Which is odd, for peace was never something Master Marlowe seemed to value.

I said a prayer for his soul. And I told him I did not

bear any grudge against him for the peril he had drawn me into. He had saved my life once—for I do not doubt I would have died or worse, had he not plucked me out of the London streets. I suppose, then, if he risked my life in the end, that made us no worse than even.

A few days after I had been taken on as Master Green's apprentice, I performed one last service for my old master. It was easy enough to find out from Master Henslowe where Master Shakespeare lodged. I sought him out on a Sunday, when there was no performance at the playhouse.

Master Shakespeare rented rooms above an ordinary. The smells of food in the kitchen—savory pork stewing with apples and spice—made my mouth water. But when I asked the landlord whether Master Shakespeare were at home, the look he gave me curdled my stomach and took my pleasure away.

"The playmaker? Aye, he's above." His smile was slow and oily, as if his teeth had been greased. "And when thou hast finished thine errand with him, come and spend some time here, sweet thing, wilt thou?"

My cheeks flamed. As Richard, no one would have thought to question me if I delivered a message to a gentleman's lodgings. But now I was Rosalind, and had to face the leer of such a man as this to run a simple errand. That was the price I paid for laying aside my breeches and doublet.

"I'd rather spend some time in the pit of hell," I said crisply, and gave him back the "thou," as contemptuous from my lips as it had been lascivious from his. "Thinkst thou the saddest draggle of a stew would kiss a man with teeth like thine?" Indeed, the man did have such a mouthful of rotten teeth as I had rarely seen, black and grayish yellow. "I hope thou dost not breathe in the taproom; thou'lt spoil the ale a-brewing."

The landlord reddened and scowled as the other men at the tables laughed, but he turned away from me with a look that made me think I'd nothing worse to fear from him. I climbed the steps toward Master Shakespeare's lodgings and knocked.

Master Shakespeare opened the door with a book in his hand, his thumb between the pages to mark his place.

"Good day, master," I said, bobbing my knee and head in a quick curtsey. "I have something that was entrusted to me. I was told it belongs to you."

"Indeed?" Master Shakespeare said, polite but puzzled. "And what may that be?"

In one hand I had the manuscript I'd rescued from Master Marlowe's rooms, the crumpled pages smoothed and stacked and neatly bound with cord. I held it out to him.

He took it, slipped the knot loose, fanned through the pages, and then glanced at me in surprise. "This is—how came thee by this?"

"My cousin gave it to me, sir. His name was Richard Archer," I answered. "He had to return to his village, but he asked me to bring it safely to you."

"I did not think to see this again." Master Shakespeare rolled the pages up and held them tenderly, as though he had something both fragile and breathing in his hands. Then he reached into his purse and pulled out a penny for me. "I thank you for your pains." He dropped another coin into my hand. "And if you see your cousin, will you tell him that he has my gratitude as well?"

The second penny did not startle me half as much as the respectful "you." For a moment I thought it might be simple carelessness, but when I glanced up at the play-maker's thoughtful face, I dismissed that idea quickly. I knew this was not a man to use words carelessly.

I closed my hand on the coins and bobbed my head again. "I thank you, sir. If I see my cousin, I'll tell him what you say."

"Do so." He smiled at me. "May I know your name, who has restored my property to me?"

"Rosalind Archer, master."

"Rosalind. A fair name. And live you here in London?"

"Yes, master. I work at the Rose playhouse. I am the tireman's apprentice."

"Then we shall see each other again, I have no doubt." He gave me a slight but courtly bow. "Farewell."

Summer has come to the city again, and I am off once more for Deptford. Master Green has given me leave to go and ask if there is any news of Will's ship. It is early yet, but not impossible some word of her safe passage to the New World might have reached home, although Will himself cannot be back again for many months. Perhaps my hair will have grown out before he returns.

They know who I am at the playhouse, of course. They are too familiar with illusion to be easily deceived. But they do not mention it, just as they do not mention Master Marlowe's death as anything but a sad accident, a tragedy of drink and quick tempers and knives too easily to hand. To the players and Master Henslowe I am Rosalind, Robin's cousin from the country. Richard Archer, so far as anyone knows, went back to his home village after the sad death of his master.

I miss Richard at times. I miss the freedom to walk briskly without my skirts tangling around my ankles. I miss the ease with which he slipped unnoticed through a crowd. A woman is always visible; a woman at the playhouse, that den of sin and shamelessness, draws more than her share of attention.

But I find I'm not afraid. I know my way around London now. I never get lost. This trade that seemed like a prison to Will Green fits me like a nest fits a swallow. I have what I thought I'd never have again once my father died. Tireman's apprentice, player's sister. I have a place.

I wonder what Will might say to me when he comes sailing home?

a note about history

Christopher Marlowe was the most successful playwright of his time, more famous than the young Shakespeare. His plays were spectacular affairs, full of gorgeous costumes, exotic settings, battles, swordfights, and lots of blood. It's also likely that Marlowe was a spy for the Elizabethan government. Under Henry VIII, and later under his daughter, Queen Elizabeth, it became illegal to practice the Catholic faith in England. When she first came to the throne, Elizabeth tended to be lenient with her Catholic subjects, but as her reign went on, penalties and persecution became more severe. One of Marlowe's jobs for her intelligence service may have been to inform on secret Catholics and priests.

In the London of Marlowe's day, there were many immigrants from Holland, and as immigrants often are, they were the targets of suspicion and prejudice. On May 5, 1593, a libel, or poster, was pasted up on the wall of a London church where most Dutch immigrants worshipped, calling on Londoners to attack their Dutch neighbors. No one knew who had written the libel, but it referred to three of Marlowe's plays, including *The Massacre at Paris* and *Tamburlaine.*

Not long after this incident, Marlowe was killed in Deptford, a port near London. Robert Pooley, another spy, was present at his death and gave testimony at the inquest. The official verdict was self-defense in a fight that arose over the bill, but theories have abounded ever since as to who was actually responsible for the death of London's best-known playmaker.

Robert Cecil was a member of the queen's Privy Council, which handled the day-to-day business of the English government. He did indeed write secretly to King James VI of Scotland, promising him help and support in the matter of the succession, although there is no evidence that he did so as early as 1592. If Queen Elizabeth had ever discovered these letters, Cecil would have been convicted of treason.

a note about language

The English that the Elizabethans spoke was not too different from what we speak today. There are some words we've stopped using; most people nowadays wouldn't know that a picadil is a roll of fabric at the shoulder of a shirt or that a maltworm is someone who drinks too much. And we've added some new words, like "nanosecond" and "ecology." But if you met an Elizabethan, you could probably understand each other, more or less.

There is, however, one major difference between the English of today and the English of the sixteenth century: the pronoun "thou" (and "thee," which is the objective form of "thou"). When we are talking directly to someone, we always use the pronoun "you." Elizabethans also used "you." But they used "thou" as well.

Deciding whether to use "you" or "thou" could be a tricky question for an Elizabethan. Here are some of the rules.

"You" is always used for the plural. Anyone speaking to more than one person would say "you."

"You" is also used to speak to a single person who's considered more important than you are. A child talking to an adult, a servant to a master, or a peasant to a nobleman would say "you."

"Thou" is used to speak to someone considered less important than you. An adult talking to a child, a master to a servant, or a nobleman to a peasant would say "thou." "Thou" can even be used to insult somebody. If you're talking to an acquaintance or a stranger of your social rank or better, you can call that person "thou" if you're really angry. But you'd better be prepared for a fight.

You can also use "thou" if you're talking to someone you love and feel close to. Lovers, siblings, and close friends can call each other "thou."

"Thou" comes with its own set of verb endings that we don't use anymore in modern English. Usually an "st" or "est" ending is paired with a "thou." So you might say "How dost thou?" to your servant or sibling or dear friend, but "How do you?" to your parent, employer, or a duke you happened to meet in passing.